SOFT HANDS

TRIPPING - BOOK 1

ARIEL BISHOP

For all the people who told me they wanted to read this story
and who fell in love with Jordan and Xander along with me.
This one's for you!

CONTINENTAL HOCKEY LEAGUE

New England Division

Baltimore Basilisks
Providence Griffins
Boston Banshees
New York Gargoyles
New Jersey Reapers
Toronto Trolls
Ottawa Sirens
Montreal Manticores

Seaboard Division

Carolina Chimeras
Miami Hellhounds
Pensacola Hydras
Philadelphia Phantoms
Washington Wyverns
Atlanta Krakens
Nashville Nagas
Kansas City Centaurs

Heartland Division

Wisconsin Wendigos
Texas Thunderbirds
Chicago Wizards
New Mexico Jackalopes
Detroit Sphinxes
Colorado Yetis
Alberta Abominables
Montana Werewolves

Gold Coast Division

Seattle Selkies
Vegas Vampires
Portland Sasquatches

Arizona Phoenixes

Los Angeles Chupacabras

San Jose Dragons

Idaho Giants

Vancouver Leviathans

WISCONSIN WENDIGOS LINEUP

Forwards

First Line
Xander "Richie" Richards - Left
David "Sonny" Dickson - Center (C)
Agustin "Becks" Zubeck

Second Line
Chan "Singer" Hsing - Left
Josh "Harty" Hartsburg - Center
Andrew "Molly" Yermolayev - Right

Third Line
Adam "Huffs" Hufford - Left
Arthur "Shinny" Mishin - Center
Paul "Deelio" Deel - Right

Fourth Line

Daniel "Yo" Portillo - Left
Roger "Haircut" Barbour - Center
Jamie "Parks" Parker - Right
Fifth Line
Timothy "Annie" Scanian - Left
Jeffrey "Beans" Rice - Center
Tony "Mary" Mariano - Right

Defense

First Pair
Aleksandr "Sasha" Ivanov (A)
Dalton "Elvis - Presby
Second Pair
Samir "Dino" Medina
Rodion "Niki" Kolesnikov
Third Pair
Patrick "Ake" Akesson
Ian "Danny" McDaniel
Fourth Pair
Ron "Silver" Silvey
Ivan "Rosie" Rosario

Goalies

Bo "Mac" MacAllister (A)

Henrik "Ricky" Pohjonen
Lucas "LK" King

Utility

Adriano "Ads" Cruz (D)
Oscar "Baldy" Baldwin (F)
Seth "Con" Connolly (F)
Liam "Mal" Malbrough (D)
Aiden "Ray" Reynolds (F)
Mitchell "Jacks" Jackson (F)

1

XANDER

Xander wakes up to light streaming in through his windows, pale and earlier than he likes to see on days when he doesn't have practice. He stretches slowly, eyes still closed. The pleasant twinges in his muscles and the warmth of the bodies on either side of him match up with his memories of last night and bring a smile to his face.

He opens his eyes when the hand on his chest starts to move, sliding slowly over the trail of of hair leading downward. "Morning," he says softly.

"Mmm," Braden--no, wait, Aiden--murmurs back, his lips curving up into a smile as his hand moves lower. "Sure is. I see someone's awake."

Xander sucks in a breath as Aiden's hand wraps

confidently around his morning wood, sliding the foreskin slowly up and down. "Every damn day."

Aiden's smile widens as he leans in for a kiss, tongue slipping confidently into Xander's mouth. He's distracting enough, between his mouth and his hands, that it takes Xander a minute to remember what he wanted to ask.

"Should we--" he cuts his eyes to his other side where Aiden's girlfriend--what was her name-- Amanda? Ashley?--lay sleeping, light brown curls spread over the pillow.

"Nah." Aiden ducked his head to nibble his way down Xander's neck. "Ash isn't a morning person. Besides, she got to blow you last night. It's my turn."

Xander brings his hand up to thread through Aiden's dark hair, a shiver running down his spine. "Not gonna say no to that. Condoms in the drawer."

He braces for argument, but Aiden just shifts enough to tug the drawer open, foil and cardboard rustling as he rummages for a condom, his other hand still stroking teasingly up and down Xander's cock.

Once he has the condom in hand, Aiden doesn't waste any time, ripping the packet open with his teeth and rolling the latex down Xander's cock. He slides down between Xander's legs, looking up at him from under dark lashes as he closes his mouth over the head.

Xander does his best to keep quiet, but Aiden is enthusiastic and practiced, his mouth hot and tight and glorious around Xander's cock. "Fuck, yes," he breathes, his hand tightening in Aiden's hair. "Just like--fuck--just like that."

Aiden moans at the tugs on his hair, the sound vibrating around Xander's cock and sending sensation shooting down his spine.

"You like that?" Xander pants, doing it again and getting an emphatically affirmative moan for his trouble.

Ashley groans next to him, stretching elaborately. "It's not bad enough you woke me up, you have to wake me up with bad porn dialogue?"

"Classic for--fuck--a reason," Xander shoots back with a smile, reaching over with his free hand to push her hair back from her face. "Can I make it up to you?"

"You'd fucking better," she retorts, smiling when she leans in for a kiss.

Xander licks into her mouth, moaning a little into the kiss and thrusting up helplessly into

Aiden's mouth. He maintains enough presence of mind to trail his hand down Ashley's body, teasing at her nipples, skimming over her stomach and sliding down between her legs where she's already slick and wet.

He plays with her clit until she's squirming, her hips rolling up helplessly, before sliding lower and pushing a finger slowly inside her pussy. The angle is bad, though; his wrist starts aching after a few minutes and he can't get as deep as he wants.

"C'mere," he says, urging her up. "Come sit on my face. I didn't get to eat you out last night."

Ashley flushes, but with a little more urging, she grips the headboard for balance and swings a leg over to straddle his face.

Xander curls his hands around her hips, pulls her down to bury his face in her pussy, and devotes every last bit of attention he has left to the task at hand. It's been awhile since he's eaten a girl out, but he hasn't entirely lost his touch, judging from the noises Ashley makes as he licks up her center, alternating between fucking his tongue inside her and licking at her clit. Even if he is distracted by the hot suction of Aiden's mouth around his cock.

He's actually grateful for the muffling effect of the condom and the way it extends his stamina. As it is, his moans as he comes are what send Ashley over the edge, her body shaking above him.

He watches, awash in the contented aftermath of a good orgasm, as Aiden retrieves another condom and coaxes Ashley back down to the bed, arranging her on her hands and knees before fucking into her. They move together like they've been doing it for years--for all he knows, Xander realizes, they have. As hot as last night was--Ashley writhing on Xander's cock while Aiden opened him up, then fucked him--there was always the edge of unfamiliarity, the slight missteps that come when you're learning what a new partner likes or doesn't like.

What's happening right now is different. It's objectively hot, no denying that. Even though he just came, Xander can acknowledge that it's an arousing sight—the flex of Aiden's fingers on her hips, his cock disappearing into her pussy, the way her body arches into his every thrust. But more than that, it's like watching two lineys who are incredibly in sync. They just--fit together.

Fortunately they both come before Xander can think about that too closely.

"AND BREAKFAST, TOO?" Ashley asks, pulling her hair into a ponytail as she comes out of the bedroom. "This is absolutely the classiest threesome ever."

"Satisfaction guaranteed." Xander throws a grin over his shoulder as he turns the bacon. He'd slipped into his oldest, softest sweatpants after the shower, not bothering with a shirt, and left Ashley and Aiden to sort out their clothes while he started breakfast. "Have a seat, it'll be done in like five minutes."

She slips onto one of the stools at the breakfast bar. "You know, you don't have to. A lot of guys would've already had us in a cab."

Xander shrugs. "I'm not a lot of guys."

"I can see that," she murmurs, and maybe he preens a little. But he works hard on his body; is it a crime to enjoy it when others appreciate the results?

"Hey, bacon!" Aiden buttons his shirt as he steps into the living area, rolling up the sleeves over what are, objectively, really nice forearms.

Xander mentally congratulates past him on having excellent taste. "And eggs. Have a seat; it'll be ready soon."

"You sure we can't do anything?" Aiden asks, kissing Ashley absently as he comes into reach.

"Nope," Xander says cheerfully, turning away and checking the bacon before he realizes he just flipped it. "Not a thing. Just sit there and keep me company."

They make quiet small talk while Xander flips the bacon out onto a plate covered in paper towels and cracks eggs into the skillet. It's all perfectly pleasant, and if there's the occasional slight edge of awkwardness, it's completely understandable, given that Xander only met them last night. And that most of their time spent together hadn't involved a lot of talking.

Once breakfast is over, Aiden and Ashley insist on helping to clear the dishes, and Xander insists on calling them a Lyft, no matter how many times they tell him it's not necessary.

"Fine," Aiden finally sighs.

Xander tries to hide his triumphant smile, tapping at his phone screen. "It'll be here in five minutes."

"This was fun," Ashley says brightly, standing on tiptoe to kiss him on the cheek. "If you ever want to do it again--"

"Sure," he says easily.

She looks at him for a moment, then smiles a little sadly. "Not really into repeats, huh?"

"It's not--"

Her finger cuts him off, pressing against his lips. "It's okay. You don't have to explain. We had fun. No hard feelings."

"You're not gonna read about this on Dead-spin," Aiden adds, leaning in for his own cheek kiss.

Xander stares at him, mouth hanging open in the way that always makes him look like a confused fish.

"Dude, you're not exactly incognito," Aiden says. "Besides, we're both big Wendigos fans. We met at a game."

The vibration of Xander's phone saves him from having to figure out what the correct response is to that statement. "Your Lyft is here."

Ashley laces her fingers through Aiden's and pulls him toward the door. "Seriously though, Xander. It was great. Ten out of ten, would fuck again."

He's still laughing when the door closes behind them.

"HEY, MAN," Justin says when the call connects, leaning back in his recliner. "What's up?"

"Not much." Xander stretches out on his couch, warmth blooming in his chest. "Last day before training camp, you know. Just enjoying the laziness."

Justin rolls his eyes. "Whatever, asshole. Like you didn't run five miles yesterday. Plus whatever extracurricular activity you were up to last night."

They've been friends for too long for Xander to be this surprised by Justin's perceptiveness, even if they aren't lineys anymore, but somehow he still is. "How did you know about last night?"

"Well, you always look more relaxed after you get laid, and Mac told me a bunch of you went out last night." Justin smirks, which is, as always, just unfair. "But the real giveaway was the Pluto-sized hickey you're rocking."

Xander's face heats and he claps a hand to the side of his neck reflexively. "Yeah, yeah, whatever. Some of us aren't happily married and have to get our rocks off however we can."

"Disgustingly happily married," Justin corrects, the smirk widening to a smug grin. "And oh no, poor Xander Richards, has to fuck his way through the single population of Milwaukee just to give his right hand a break. Who was it this time. Guy? Girl?"

"Try one of each," Xander shoots back, flipping his friend off with said right hand. "A nice couple looking to get a little crazy."

Justin shakes his head. "Only you, man. One of these days you're gonna get tired of this hookup shit and settle down, though."

"Nah." Xander does his best to ignore the tightness in his chest, the same as every other time Justin brings this shit up. "You married the last perfect woman. I'm gonna be single forever."

"It's true," Justin says, his smile going so sloppy and affectionate that Xander can't maintain any kind of resentment, no matter how much he tries. Seeing Justin happy is basically his Kryptonite; he's just had to accept it. "Brooke says hi, by the way."

Xander rolls his eyes. "Hi back. When are you two going to give me godchildren?"

"You sound like my mom. First of all, we've only been married for six months, and second, what makes you think we'd let you be the godfather?"

"I'd be a fucking awesome godfather."

It's Justin's turn to roll his eyes. "Yeah, you'd teach them to say 'fucking.' With our luck it'd be their first word."

Xander shrugs. "Could be worse and you know

it. Can you imagine the kind of shit Elvis would say around a kid?"

"Oh shit," Justin groans. "New rule; I have to retire before we have kids. Can't raise them around hockey players, that's for fucking sure."

"Like you're any fucking better."

They sit there in silence for a few minutes, just grinning at each other through the Skype window. "Fuck, I miss you," Justin says finally.

"That's gay," Xander retorts, trying to ignore the aching twist in his gut.

"You're bi, asshole. And so am I. Quit calling things gay like it's an insult."

Xander waves a dismissive hand. "Yeah, yeah. I miss you, too. For some dumb reason."

Whatever Justin was going to say next is interrupted by Brooke's voice, muffled but still audible. "Is that Xander?"

"Yeah." Justin's whole face goes soft, the way it never does when he looks at Xander. "Come say hi, babe."

Brooke enters the camera, sliding into Justin's lap. "Hey! How's my favorite forward?"

"Hey!"

"Just being lazy." Xander raises his voice to talk over Justin, who is apparently distracting himself from his outrage by nuzzling into the side of Brooke's neck. "Training camp tomorrow, so I have to really soak it in. How's school going? Have you started back yet?"

She shakes her head, ignoring Justin with the ease of long practice. Or appearing to. "Two more beautiful, homework-free weeks. And as soon as this jackass starts his training camp, I might actually get some time to myself instead of having him demanding attention all the damn time."

"He's like a puppy," Xander agrees, smiling when Justin opens his mouth to protest. "At least you finally got him house-trained."

Brooke grins back, sighing theatrically. "Only barely."

"I resent this conversation," Justin announces, nudging the strap of Brooke's tank top off her shoulder and kissing the bared skin. "Richie, love you, man, but I'm gonna shut this down and go have sex with my wife."

"Justin!"

Xander shakes his head; he has no idea why Brooke bothers acting surprised. Or appalled. The two of them have never been able to keep their hands off each other. At least now he doesn't have to listen to them fuck on the other side of his bedroom wall. "Don't let me stop you, bro. Do what you gotta do."

"Oh, I will."

The last thing Xander sees before the screen goes black is Justin's wicked grin, his hand pushing the hem of Brooke's tank top up to expose the smooth, soft skin of her stomach.

It's all too easy for his stupid, treacherous brain to fill in the rest of the picture. He's seen Justin and Brooke kissing too many times to count, the way they lean into each other, lips meeting and parting. Are they undressing right there in Justin's recliner, too desperate for each other to move to a different location? Is Brooke grinding down on Justin's cock, making him groan in the back of his throat, the noise Xander always pretended he hadn't heard through their shared wall back when they'd lived in the same apartment.

You're not doing this, he tells himself sternly. *You're not jerking off to your married best friend. Not again. You just had a fucking threesome, asshole. Quit thinking with your dick.*

But that—that's worse. Because now his brain has latched onto that idea, flooding him with full-color, three dimensional memories of the night before. Only instead of the random couple he picked up, it's Brooke spread out under him as he thrusts into her hot, wet pussy. It's Justin's fingers opening him up, torturously teasing, Justin's voice in his ear.

Xander shoves his sweats down, groaning with relief when he gets a hand around his cock. It's wrong, he knows, and worse, it's stupid. But he's long since accepted that he's stupid in love with Justin, even if nothing will ever come of it. Next time, next time he'll be stronger, smarter. He'll resist. But this is the only way he'll ever have this with Justin, only ever in his imagination. And really, no one ever said Xander was smart.

"GREEDY," Justin mock-chides, curling his fingers to brush teasingly over Xander's prostate. "Think you're ready, Xan?"

"Yes," Xander pants, grinding back, trying to get Justin's fingers deeper, harder. "Come on, Justin, fuck me already."

Justin chuckles, adding a third finger so slowly that all Xander can do is breathe through the stretch, almost whining.

"Please," he breathes, not caring how it sounds, not

caring about anything except getting Justin's cock inside him. "Please, fuck me, please—"

"Well, since you asked so nicely," Justin teases. "What do you think, baby? Think I should give him what he wants?"

Brooke hums consideringly. "He's been pretty good. I think he deserves it."

Xander shoots her a grateful look, redoubling his efforts to make her come again. He's still intensely aware of Justin's fingers, thrusting in and out before they're suddenly gone, leaving him empty and aching.

Not for long, though. Seconds later he can feel the blunt pressure of Justin's cock pressing against him, pushing slowly, inexorably inside. "Yeah," he groans, doing his best to breathe, to bear down and accept it. "Oh fuck, yeah."

"So fucking tight." Justin's voice is tense, his fingers flexing on Xander's hips. "Fuck, Xan, you feel so good."

Xander would feel guilty for neglecting Brooke, every bit of attention he has to spare focused on the feeling of Justin fucking him, but she's moaning under him, little breathy sounds as Justin's every thrust pushes Xander's cock into her pussy.

"I'm close," she whimpers, her fingers digging into Xander's biceps as she rolls her hips up to meet his— Justin's—thrusts. "Babe—Xan—please, fuck—"

"We got you," Justin soothes, pressing his mouth to Xander's neck as he bottoms out. "Don't we, Xan?"

Somehow Xander manages an affirmative noise, following Justin's rhythm. It's overwhelming, his cock surrounded by wet, tight heat, his ass spread open for the hard, hot length of Justin's cock. He holds on to control with his fingernails, but when Brooke comes, tightening down around his cock, he can't hold back any longer, thrusting erratically inside her until he comes, too.

They're both moaning, shuddering messes, clinging to each other as Justin speeds up, chasing his own orgasm. When he comes with a muttered, "Fuck—love you—" Xander knows it's not meant for him.

But it's so easy to pretend.

XANDER LOOKS DOWN AT HIMSELF, sweats shoved down to mid-thigh, his hand and chest covered with cooling semen. Part of him wants to stay right there, tells him he doesn't deserve anything better. What kind of a scumbag asshole jerks off thinking about a threesome with his best friend? What kind of idiot falls in love with his best friend, keeps twisting the knife even when his best friend is happily married? Something must be broken inside him, that he can't get over this, can't feel this way for anyone else, no matter how hard he tries

He forces himself up off the couch and into the shower for the second time that day. He might be a broken scumbag idiot asshole, but at least he can be a clean one.

And if he spends the rest of the day curled up in his bed watching trashy reality TV, well, it's the last day before training camp. He can be lazy if he wants. It has nothing to do with the ache in his chest.

Nothing at all.

2

JORDAN

"Nana, I'm gonna have to go," Jordan says, buttoning his work-issued polo shirt. "It's the first day of training camp and if I don't leave in like five minutes I'll get stuck in traffic."

"Oh, all right." Even the slight tinniness of the phone speaker can't hide the amusement in her voice. "Go off to your big fancy CHL job. Just try to spare some time to call your poor old Nana, all alone down here with no grandchildren to cuddle."

Jordan snorts. "Oh, please. You go out more than I do. Tell me you don't have like five places to be today."

"Gotta fill my time somehow," Nana shoots

back. "When are you gonna settle down with a nice boy and adopt some babies?"

"The season's about to start, Nana." Jordan rubbed a hand over his head, feeling the close-cropped hair prickle against his palm. "You know I want that, but this is just my third year here. I need to focus on my career right now, not finding a boyfriend. Besides, it's hard to date when I'm working basically every Friday and Saturday night."

He can practically hear Nana rolling her eyes, even over the phone. "That sounds like an excuse. Anyway, you kids these days think dating is everything. Sometimes the right person just comes out of nowhere. You just have to be ready."

"Look, you know I want that." Jordan swallows around the sudden tightness in his throat. "And someday, I promise. Husband, kids, the whole shebang. Just—not right now."

"Just promise me you'll be ready," Nana says, her voice unusually gentle. "You don't want to look back later and realize you let a good thing get away from you."

He swallows again. "Yeah, I promise."

"Good boy," she says briskly. "Now I promised Eileen I'd go down to the senior center with her, so

I'll let you get to work. You just remember what I told you, now, you hear? I love you, Jordan."

"Love you, too."

Jordan tucks his phone into his shorts pocket after he hangs up and goes in search of his keys, trying to ignore the ache of homesickness in his chest. Not for the heat of Baton Rouge, the bugs, the slap of humidity when you step outside. But for a second, he can almost see his Nana's house, the wood floors and the sunlight streaming in through the windows.

He can't remember living with his parents very well, everything before the accident a blur with only a few specific memories. Home was always Nana's house, the smell of gumbo and red beans and rice, the whir of the ceiling fan and the sound of music over the little radio she kept in the kitchen. Maybe he didn't have a bunch of brothers and sisters and cousins running around like most of the other kids in the neighborhood, but he'd known every day, that he was loved.

Sometimes it feels ungrateful to wish for more, to fantasize about a husband and a house full of kids. But right now, he realizes as he catches sight of the clock on the oven, he needs to get his ass in gear if he's not going to be late for work. Like he'd told Nana, time enough for that later.

JORDAN BREATHES deep as he steps inside the arena. It always smells the same—industrial cleaners, the lingering undertones of sweat, and the clean, cold smell of the ice even this far from the rink. Something in him settles at the indisputable evidence that he's back where he belongs. Not that the off-season hadn't been nice; working with private clients and having a much less rigorous schedule was a great change. But it's good to be back.

He valiantly ignores the little voice in the back of his head that says there's a particular reason he's glad to be back. That the little curl of excitement and nerves in his stomach has nothing to do with starting a new season and everything to do with seeing a particular forward for the first time in months.

You are a grown-ass man, he tells himself as he follows the hallway toward the trainers' room. *You are too old for this idiot crush business. He's a member of the team. Be a goddamn professional.*

"Hey, stranger." Marian looks up from her desk as he comes into the shared trainers' office. "You ready to whip these assholes into shape?"

"I'm ready to stand behind you and let you do it," Jordan grins back at her, tucking his laptop bag under his desk. "You know you're gonna have to step on a rookie or two before the rest get the message. We might as well start early."

She rolls her eyes. "Yeah, yeah. You're just lazy, Jordy. That's your problem."

"I don't see you offering to massage twenty Achilles tendons and thirteen rotator cuffs," he retorts.

Before she can come up with a response, Johnson sticks his head in the door. "Oh good, you're both here. Coach White wants a meeting before the players get here. His office, five minutes."

He barely waits for their acknowledgment before he's back out the door.

"Well, here we go," Marian sighs, pushing herself out of her chair. "Let's go earn that fat CHL paycheck."

WHEN JORDAN and the rest of the staff make it

into the meeting room, the players are already milling around. The veterans are backslapping and chatting, gathered into clumps, while the rookies stand wide-eyed, usually with their backs to the wall, trying to pretend they're all casual.

Jordan curses himself for the way he's scanning the crowd of players for a head of light brown hair, even more when a familiar laugh draws his attention like metal to a magnet. And seriously, fuck Xander Richards, because the asshole somehow managed to get even more attractive in the two months since Jordan saw him last. He clearly didn't bother to shave this morning, because he's a public fucking menace. The morning light glints gold off his stubble as he throws his head back and laughs again, lips parting over slightly crooked teeth.

Fuck. Jordan looks away too late, the image seared into his mind like he's spent too long staring at the sun.

Coach White steps up to the podium, one hand raised to get the players' attention, thankfully saving Jordan from any further contemplation of his hopeless, stupid crush and the ridiculous similes he has to resort to. The welcome and staff introductions are, as usual, mercifully brief. Before he knows it, Jordan's caught up in the swing of training camp, manning his stations and making sure none of these idiots injure themselves on the first day. Oh, and watching Marian effortlessly flatten the few rookies stupid enough to think that because she's a woman, she doesn't know what she's talking about.

"Only two this year," he says to her at lunch. "Are they getting smarter?"

She shrugs. "Maybe. Or maybe I'm just getting meaner. What was that with Richards?"

Jordan thanks every deity he's ever heard of that his skin is too dark to show a blush. "Huh?"

"Remember how we agreed I'm getting meaner?" The look she levels on him makes him feel maybe twelve years old again, even though they're basically the same age. "Don't try to bullshit me, Darling. He was flirting with you."

"Xander flirts with everybody," he says quietly, his eyes on his chicken.

It's true, and she knows it. As much as Jordan would like to think that he's special, that the casual touching, the sideways glances, the way Xander's voice curls around Jordan's last name like it's actually an endearment means anything—it doesn't. Anybody who's been with the team for more than a month has ample evidence of that, in the parade of men and women in and out of Xander's bed.

Xander Richards doesn't do serious. *Probably the only thing he doesn't do,* Jordan thinks, hating himself a little for the snideness of it, even though it's true.

Marian hums skeptically, but when he shoots her a pleading look, she lets it go.

The universe must be trying to apologize for something, because Mårtensson leans over to ask her something about one of the rookies and Jordan is able to finish his lunch in peace. Well, as much peace as he can find when he's back to daily contact with Xander.

It'll get better, he tells himself silently. *You'll get used to it, you'll get over it. It'll get better.*

He doesn't believe it.

It's a relief to escape into the trainers room after lunch. This is the part Jordan's best at; he freely admits that his skills for handling large groups of players need work, even though he knows his stuff. But here, one-on-one? This is what he's good at.

Hartsburg is the first player in, basically throwing himself full length on the massage table like the giant drama queen he is. "I'm gonna die," he moans, his voice muffled against the vinyl surface. "Kill me now."

"Knee again?" Jordan asks cheerfully, his hands already feeling out the muscles in Hartsburg's thigh, the quadricep knotted tight and rock-hard to the touch. "Did you do your PT at all this summer?"

"I swear I did." Hartsburg groans when Jordan's fingers find a particularly tender spot. "All those fucking stretches. I was so good. And now I'm gonna die. "

Jordan rolls his eyes. "You're not going to die. You might wish you had after the next couple of minutes, though."

"I can take it."

"That's the spirit." Jordan digs his knuckles into the muscles, maybe smiling a little when Hartsburg nearly yells from it. "Gonna cry?"

Hartsburg grits his teeth. "No."

"Good." Jordan keeps up the pressure. "If you cry, you owe me a tip."

"Mother*fucker*," Hartsburg hisses. "You have fucking Wolverine claws, dude, what the fuck."

Jordan shakes his head. "Fortify, Harty. Almost got it."

"Hey, you got room for me, Darling?"

"On the other table," Jordan says shortly,

pretending he hadn't nearly jumped out of his skin at the sound of his name in that familiar, low voice. He's aware, all too aware, of Xander moving around in his peripheral vision, but he forces himself to keep his fingers steady, to do his fucking job. "Be with you in a minute."

Xander chuckles, the vinyl table cover creaking as he shifts his position. "Take your time, Darling."

Do your fucking job, Jordan repeats to himself, Narrowing his focus down to Hartsburg's leg, he forces himself to make sure every knot and trigger point is smoothed away.

Finally, though, he can't stall any more. "I think that's as good as it gets, Harty," he finally has to say. "Better get back to it."

"Thanks, Jordy," Hartsburg says brightly, flexing the muscle a couple of times before sliding down from the table. "See ya, Richie."

With that reminder, Jordan can't pretend any longer that he doesn't know what's waiting for him. But when he turns, it's so much worse than he was expecting. Xander is sitting there, casually swinging his legs like he's a five-year-old boy instead of a six-foot-one CHL player who's taken his fucking shirt off.

"I forgot you were allergic to clothes," Jordan says, doing his best not to roll his eyes again.

Xander shrugs, muscles rippling distractingly under his tattoos, stark black and gray against the pale gold of his skin. "Figured I'd save a step, unless you want to massage my shoulder through my t-shirt."

"How's your recovery been?" Jordan asks after a moment, since that seems like a safer topic than further comment on Xander's half-nakedness.

Another shrug. "Pretty good. Stuck to the PT schedule, got almost the full range of motion back. But it's a little tender. Figured I'd pop in here, avail myself of your magic hands before it gets any worse."

For the second time that day, Jordan finds himself thankful his skin is dark enough not to show the heat he feels in his cheeks. "Chest or back?"

Xander shifts his shoulders experimentally. "Huh. Both, but more back than chest."

"Well, lets get the chest first, then you can lay down," Jordan says briskly, willfully suppressing the *and stop looking at me* that tries to slip out after it.

And then there's nothing for it but to step in closer, to reach out. Xander's skin is warm under his hands, the muscle flexing, rising and falling with each breath. His pectorals are tight, and Jordan's fingers work on instinct, moving along the line of Xander's collarbone toward his deltoids, toward the faded scar that almost, from a distance, looks like part of his tattoos.

It's the best-worst kind of torture. The part of Jordan's brain that is a trained professional is basically looking in disgust at the rest of him, which apparently never matured past a fifteen-year-old with a crush on the star quarterback. It's pretty disgusting, to be honest, how much he's having to tamp down an internal freakout over the fact that he's actually touching Xander.

"Yeah, you're a little tight," Jordan says inanely, digging his thumbs into the knots and trying to keep his composure when Xander honest-to-god fucking moans at the touch.

"Fuck, how does that hurt so good?" Xander moans again, his head falling back and eyes sliding shut.

Jordan sneaks a look and immediately regrets all of his recent life choices. His stupid, traitorous imagination whispers that this is what Xander would look like during sex, completely abandoned and gorgeous and fuck Jordan's life, he *cannot* get a boner while he's working.

"Lie down on your front so I can get your shoulder." Jordan does his best not to yank his hands back like he wants to, like self-preservation is telling him to.

He's not sure how well he succeeds, but Xander obeys the order without question, settling flat onto the table in one fluid motion. His stupid, long arms dangle down off the sides, so Jordan has to pick up the one nearest to him and lay it back on the tabletop so he can work. Which he does, absolutely not resisting the urge to trace the intricate swirls of ink covering every inch of Xander's skin. Nope. Not even a little. And the Nile isn't a river in Egypt.

"Holy shit," he breathes when he gets his hands on Xander's shoulder, his stupid personal turmoil pushed aside for the moment because, all evidence to the contrary, he is actually a goddamn professional. "A little tender, huh?"

"It's no big," Xander mumbles, his voice muffled against the table. "Nothing compared to before."

Rolling his eyes feels even more juvenile, but Xander seems to bring it out in him. "Compared to a torn fucking rotator cuff? Yeah, but that doesn't mean it's minor. You can't push too hard, or you're going to fuck up your shoulder before the season even starts."

He's expecting an argument, or at least some kind of pushback, but Xander just nods. "Yeah, I know. It snuck up on me. I'll be more careful tomorrow."

"Well—good," Jordan says inanely, digging his fingers in a little harder as the surface knots start to loosen.

He can't think of anything else to say, and apparently neither can Xander, so he works in silence for a few minutes more. The lack of distraction is both a blessing and a curse, just like everything else with Xander. It gives Jordan time to notice little details that he usually tries to ignore. Xander's lashes, thick and dark and so long they brush his cheekbones when his eyes are closed. His hair, curling just slightly at the nape of his neck, glints of red and gold in the sandy brown. His shoulders, broadly muscled and tapering down to a narrow waist.

It's tempting to linger, but Jordan is all too aware that any of the other players or coaching staff could walk in at any time. The last thing he needs is Marian asking more probing questions. He can justify working on Xander's other shoulder and his lower back, because the tension has spread, but eventually he has to lift his hands and say "I think that'll do it."

Xander's eyes flutter open and he slowly pushes himself up to a sitting position. "Holy shit, man," he says, rotating his shoulder. "Seriously, magic fucking hands."

Jordan forces his hand down from where it was rubbing at the back of his neck. "Just doing my job."

"Hey." Xander reaches for his shirt but doesn't put it back on immediately. "Are you doing anything Friday?"

"Just camp," Jordan says, a little confused.

Xander shakes his head, the corners of his lips curling up. "I meant after. Can I maybe buy you a drink? Dinner?"

It takes Jordan a minute to realize what's happening, because it's so unprecedented. But when he does, it hits him like a ton of bricks. Xander is asking him out. *Xander Richards* is *asking him out.* What the *actual fuck.*

His stupid, stupid mouth is opening to say yes when his common sense takes over. Because yes, Xander is asking him out. Xander "One-Night

Stand" Richards. Jordan's only been with the Wendigos for a couple of years, but it didn't take even a fraction of that time for him to realize that Xander isn't exactly a commitment kind of guy. All of his partners seem perfectly satisfied with the state of affairs, but Jordan hasn't seen any of them twice.

And that—that's not him. As much as part of him is screaming to take what he can get, Jordan is pretty sure even Xander's dick isn't worth the aftermath. Seeing him every day, knowing what it's like to fuck him, to get almost, almost enough—

"No thanks," he says, forcing the words out through a throat that keeps trying to close on them.

Xander looks surprised. Of course he does. Who the fuck tells Xander Richards no? But he takes it with good grace, shrugging into his shirt and pulling it down over his stupid rippling abs. "That's cool. Better get back out there before Coach sends out a search party, huh?"

"Yeah, probably," Jordan mumbles, avoiding eye contact.

Xander leaves quickly, thank fuck, nearly bumping into Presby and McAllister on their way in. Jordan spends the rest of the day almost too busy to think. Almost.

He made the right decision; he knows that. He

deserves better than to be another notch on Xander's bedpost, than to have to deal with the fallout of a one-night-stand, the awkwardness. God knows if it comes down to the choices of a trainer-slash-massage therapist or one of their first-line wingers, seventh overall draft pick Xander Richards—well, Jordan doesn't need a crystal ball to know how that will go.

It was the right decision. It was. Faced with the same situation again, he'd do the same thing. He knows this.

But when he gets home, his apartment echoing and empty around him, well. It seems less certain.

And if he lies awake that night, staring at the ceiling—if he eventually gives in, curls his hand around his cock, and pretends things were different, that he said yes, that Xander was in his bed at this moment—

"Fuck," Xander moans, reaching behind him to pull Jordan closer. "Fuck, right there—"

"Like that?" Jordan fucks up into him, palm pressed flat against his stomach to feel the muscles clench there. "That what you want?"

Xander whines as Jordan gets a hand on his cock. "Fuck, please, Jordan. I'm so close, please—"

"Gonna come for me?" Jordan pants. He can't

coordinate enough to really move his hand, but Xander seems just fine with the way Jordan's thrusts move him. "Come on, let me see it—"

"Fuck," Xander moans. His voice goes choked and breathy when he comes, his ass so tight around Jordan's cock that he can't help but come too.

Jordan blinks up at the ceiling, still slightly stupid from the force of his orgasm. All too soon, though, the pleasant warmth fades, replaced with something that feels suspiciously like shame. Is it unethical to jerk off to someone you turned down?

He rolls onto his side, pulling the covers up over him. Whatever. No one has to know.

3

XANDER

Xander hadn't meant to say it. Sure, he's noticed Jordan. Hard not to notice him; the dude is built like Captain America, even though his college football days are long behind him—yes, Xander googled, sue him.

But Xander's heedless, hit-on-anything-with-a-pulse days were thankfully left behind along with his teenage years, no matter what Justin likes to say. He knows better than to fuck around with teammates or team-adjacent people, so he's long since carefully filed Jordan Darling away in the "nice to look at, fun to flirt with, but that's it" category.

And he's fine with that. Honestly.

But something made him speak, even though he hadn't planned on it. Maybe the all-too-vivid memory of the ease Justin and Brooke have around each other, a comfort Xander has never had with any of his sexual partners. Maybe the way Jordan always ducks his head a little when Xander calls him by his last name. Maybe Xander went a little crazy with the relief from the pain when Jordan's hands were on him.

No matter what the cause, though, the fact is that he did it; he asked Jordan out. And once the words were out, he didn't even regret it. Sure, it might get a little awkward, but they could probably both be adults about it. Besides, Xander has a feeling that Jordan would be worth it.

In the end, though, it doesn't matter why Xander did it. Because Jordan turned him down. It still stings a little, even now, hours later. Now that Xander's home and can really think about it, can ponder the maybes and what-ifs, he realizes how much he was actually looking forward to Jordan, to getting to know more about him than his super-professional work-persona. To finding out what Jordan's like when he lets loose a little.

But that's not going to happen. No means no, and there are plenty of people around who'll say yes. It's good, honestly, that Jordan said no. Smart.

Xander might have temporarily lost his mind, but Jordan was thinking clearly, and Xander's thankful.

He is.

Honestly.

But his bed is a little cold, and despite the exhaustion of a day of intense training, it takes him longer than he'd like to fall asleep.

SO OF COURSE, the next morning Xander finds himself pulling into the parking lot behind Jordan's black Subaru. He has no idea how he knows what vehicle Jordan drives, but sure enough, Jordan steps out as Xander is pulling into his own parking space, unfolding his lean frame from the vehicle with surprising grace.

"Morning," Xander says, because he is not going to let this be weird. He's an adult, dammit. Okay, an adult who gets paid an obscene amount of money to chase a puck around the ice instead of having a real job, but still.

"Morning," Jordan says back, scrubbing a hand over his close-cropped hair. There's something off in his voice, but Xander pushes that aside, along with the question of how he knows what Jordan normally sounds like. Fake it till you make it, right?

"How's the shoulder?" Jordan asks as they fall into step heading into the arena.

Xander rolls the shoulder in question, testing. "Okay for now. We'll see what Coach has in store for us today, though."

"Well, you know where to find me," Jordan says, then ducks his head like he's bracing for a chirp. "If you need, you know, a massage, for your shoulder, if it's—"

"Darling!" Marian barks from down the hall. "Get in here!"

Jordan turns toward her, looking ridiculously grateful for the interruption. "I, uh, see you," he tosses over his shoulder as he heads away from Xander, long legs eating up the distance. "Later."

"Later," Xander echoes, amusement and disappointment warring in his chest. He drags his eyes away from contemplating the way Jordan's athletic shorts fit over his ass to find Marian giving him a flat, emotionless stare.

He learned better than to try and stare Marian down his rookie year, so he just nods and looks away, heading off to join the other players for warmups. It's stupid to feel disappointed, he reminds himself as he walks down the back hallway. Jordan said no. Nothing is going to happen between them, no matter how much that conversation read like awkward flirting. There are plenty of fish in the sea, as trite and cliche as that sounds. As soon as camp is over, he'll go out, pick up, and get laid. He'll forget all about Jordan Darling and his awkward laugh and his great ass and his stupid smile.

That's how it works. Until then, he'll just have to stay out of Jordan's way.

SO OF COURSE, for the rest of training camp, Jordan is fucking *everywhere*. Spotting weights for the bench press, his fingers brushing Xander's as he lifts the bar back onto the rack. Timing the agility drills, where Xander absolutely does not push himself a little harder than maybe he should have. And, of course, in the trainers room.

"Richards!" David barks the second time he catches Xander favoring his shoulder, sharing a quick look with Sasha. "Go get Jordy to look at that shoulder for you."

Xander opens his mouth to protest, but closes it

again and tosses his captain a salute as he skates off the ice. The whole point of this, he reminds himself as he strips off his sweaty gear, is for things to be normal, not awkward. Going to the trainers room to get his shoulder checked out is normal. He can be normal.

"Hey, Darling," he says as he comes into the room, because he's being normal, and that's what he'd normally say. Probably. He doesn't even fucking know anymore. What the fuck is happening? When did this become his life?

"Hey," Jordan says absently, not looking up from Kolesnikov's hamstrings. "Be right with you."

Xander shrugs, even though Jordan isn't looking. "No rush."

He never realized before how boring the trainers room is, how empty of anything to keep his attention from going where it shouldn't. Jordan's red polo shirt is just tight enough across his shoulders that the movement of muscle as he works is clear, flexing and shifting all the way down his very attractive forearms.

For all his quips about "magic hands," Xander doesn't think he's paid attention to Jordan's hands before, and that seems like a damn shame. They're big, which is probably the only descriptor he could have come up with before, with long, clever fingers that are currently wringing a series of damn-near pornographic noises out of Kolesnikov.

"Come on," Jordan says impatiently when Kolesnikov tries to wriggle out of his grip for the third time in as many minutes. "You get hit for a living, Niki. The more you move, the longer this takes. You know that."

"Sorry," Niki mutters into the table. "Sore."

Jordan shrugs. "It'll be worse in the morning if you don't let me do my job. Or do I need to get Richie to hold you down?"

Niki snorts, shooting Xander a dismissive glance. "Can try."

"Hey," Xander protests, but mildly. They're nearly the same height, only an inch difference, but Niki carries around a good 20-30 extra pounds of muscle. Probably more right now, coming off summer conditioning, before the grueling pace of the season starts taking its toll.

"Both of us could," Jordan says flatly, cutting off the argument before it starts. Fuck everything, that should *not* be so hot. "So lie still and let me finish."

Whatever Niki might have retorted is cut off when Jordan digs his fingers into the muscle, making him yelp. "Okay, okay," he mutters, pressing his forehead back down to the table.

They lapse back into silence after that, or mostly silence, interrupted only by Niki's almost-obscene groaning. Finally, after a torturous eternity where Xander does his best not to stare, Jordan steps back from the table, shaking out his hands.

"That should do it for today," he pronounces, watching like a hawk as Niki pushes himself to his feet. "Come back tomorrow, even if you don't think you need to."

"Da," Niki agrees, nodding to Xander as he leaves the room.

Xander's pretty sure he's not imagining the hesitation before Jordan turns toward him, twin to the uncertainty swirling in his gut. But hey, fake it till you make it, right? It's not like he can avoid Jordan; they fucking work together. The only way it would've been more difficult is if he was actually on the team. But even Xander isn't that stupid. Probably.

"What?" he asks, when Jordan just frowns confusedly at him.

"You're still dressed."

He looks down at himself, and sure enough,

he's still wearing his t-shirt. "Oops. Guess you can't really massage my shoulder through this, huh?"

Jordan shrugs. "I could, but it'd be a shitty massage. Never thought I'd see the day when I'd have to tell you to take your clothes off."

Thank fuck Xander is halfway through pulling his shirt over his head when the impact of those words hits. He takes an extra second or two to try and let his face cool down before taking it the rest of the way off, but he's pretty sure his cheeks are still pink at the least. Fortunately, or unfortunately, Jordan isn't looking at his face, eyes fixed firmly on his shoulder.

"Same as yesterday?" Jordan asks, his voice a shade too brisk. "Chest and back, but back worse?"

Xander nods. "Yeah, uh, basically the same. A little better, but Johnson told me to come see you to be safe."

"Good."

And then Jordan's hands are on him, and fuck. Xander knows how to be professional, okay? He's been playing hockey basically since he learned how to skate, he had more massages, sports and otherwise, than he can even begin to remember. He knows all about autonomic reactions, about deflecting with a laugh and a joke.

He doesn't know why this is happening.

Jordan said no, Xander moved on. That's how it works. He's never stayed stuck on someone like this before, not when there are so many attractive people out there for the fucking.

Except Justin, his traitorous brain reminds him, and fuck. This can't be another Justin situation. Justin is his best friend, and was long before Xander was stupid enough to fall in love with him. Jordan's a great guy, a super hot guy, but it's not the same. This is just because Xander has never had to keep interacting with someone after getting shot down before. Usually he leaves the bar or the club and that's that. It's the novelty of the situation.

Sure. And the Wendigos are going to be the first team this season to clinch a playoff spot.

"Go ahead and lie down so I can get your back."

Xander shakes himself out of his reverie. "Oh, yeah. Okay."

He spends the rest of the massage talking himself down, doing his best to ignore the texture of Jordan's fingertips against his skin, the sound of Jordan's breathing as he works, the fact that the noises he's making sound a lot more pornographic, to his ears at least, than Niki's.

"All done," Jordan announces after a minor eternity. "It didn't take as much work today, but you're probably going to have problems with stiffness for another couple of weeks at least, maybe the first few games of the season." He doesn't say, but both of them know that once the season gets going Xander will probably end up nursing an entirely new set of injuries.

"Thanks." Xander's voice is muffled by his shirt as he pulls it back on, feeling more naked than usual under Jordan's clinical, professional gaze. "Same time tomorrow?"

"You know where to find me," Jordan agrees. It looks for a second like he wants to say something else, but after a few seconds he gathers supplies and starts cleaning off the other table where the mark of Niki's forehead is still clear on the vinyl.

Xander can't think of anything else to say, so he leaves, hating the awkward, wrong-footed feeling. Fake it till you make it is all well and good, but he needs to make it soon, because this shit is getting old.

THE REST of camp is like that, too. Jordan is

fucking everywhere, or that's what it feels like. He's there for the training and the skating and the more training. He's there every fucking day whenever Xander has to finally cave and go get his shoulder massaged, because he's not stupid enough to fuck up his body for the sake of avoiding an awkward situation. The only place Xander can get away from him is at home, in his big echoing house.

He can't even complain properly to Justin about it, which keeps leaving weird, awkward gaps in their conversations. But Justin would, firstly, chirp the fuck out of him for not being able to get past this stupid crush or whatever. And secondly, he'd tell Brooke, and Xander would never hear the end of it. It's best to just suffer in silence until he gets over it.

So he spends every fucking night lying in his too-big bed, staring at the ceiling and counting the aches in his muscles until the Tylenol kicks in. More often than not, as tired as he is, he can't get his stupid brain to shut off. Not without giving in, without letting himself imagine what it would be like, having Jordan's big, clever hands on his body for less professional purposes.

It's ridiculous and stupid.

And it just. Keeps. Happening.

After the last day of camp they all head out to

JP's, the little hole-in-the-wall bar and grill the team adopted years ago, primarily because of how close it is to the arena. They fill up the party room in the back and overflow to the main dining area, loud and boisterous, giddy with the knowledge that they made it. This is their team, and tomorrow their preseason begins. And then the season. A new season. Where anything could happen.

Xander leans back against the bar, beer in hand, and just kind of watches. He didn't realize how weird it would feel to be here without Justin at his elbow; it was okay during camp, but he keeps half-turning to make an observation or crack a joke to someone who isn't there. And the Selkies are in a whole other fucking division, so he's not going to see Justin in person unless they meet in the playoffs.

"Hey," Presby says, leaning on the bar next to him and trying to catch the bartender's attention. "First preseason game tomorrow night. You ready, Richie?"

"Ready and willing," Xander agrees, scanning the room absently. "Gonna rip the Jackalopes a new one."

Presby nods, smacking his hand on the bartop for emphasis. "Yeah!"

He doesn't seem to have much else to say, but

mercifully for the both of them, the bartender slides him a refill and he salutes Xander with the bottle before making his way back to the table where Niki, Harty, and Scanlan are already sitting.

Xander takes advantage of his renewed solitude to scan the room. The team's arrival has chased away some of the other customers, but the owners never complain, more than happy to have large numbers of CHL athletes spending money on food and drinks on a regular basis. It's a good deal for the team, too, to have a place where they can relax and not worry so much about cell phone cameras or anything ending up on Deadspin.

Not so great for picking up someone, unless he's going to try for someone on the team or the staff. Which, Xander reminds himself, his eyes moving over the table where Jordan and Marian are talking about something, is not the plan. The plan is to find someone random, someone he can extricate himself from without trouble or awkwardness.

Someone he's not going to find here.

He drains the last of his beer and leaves the bottle on the bar with enough cash to cover his tab and a healthy tip on top of it. Lyft says he can have a ride in 2 minutes, so he taps the button and heads for the door.

He half-expects chirps or questions about leaving so soon when it seems like most of the Wendigos are settling in for a few hours. But hardly anyone seems to even notice. Not aside from a few looks from the table where David is sitting with Mac and Sasha, heads together over some sort of captain/alternate captain business. And even they quickly go back to whatever they were discussing, David pretending not to watch while Sasha's hand rubs absent circles on Mac's shoulder.

Xander shoves the slightly hollow feeling aside and ignores the urge to check and see if Jordan is watching as he walks out the door and finds his ride.

"Hey," the driver—Drew, the app informs him —says as Xander slides into the backseat. "Heading to Valentine's?"

"Yeah," Xander confirms, buckling his seatbelt. "Look, I'm not really in the mood for conversation right now. I'll double the tip if you just drive."

Drew shrugs and pulls away from the curb. "Whatever you say."

The drive is mercifully short, thank fuck; Drew slides through traffic like some kind of wizard, and less than fifteen minutes later they're double-parked outside of Valentine's. "Thanks," Xander says, stepping out of the car and pulling his phone out to tip before he forgets.

There's no line, not this early in the evening, but the dance floor is reasonably full, bodies moving more or less successfully to the low, pulsing bass line the DJ is spinning. Xander makes his way to the bar, feeling a strange sense of deja vu. He hesitates for a second over his order, but the last thing he needs is to get truly wasted the night before a game, especially since he's planning on picking up. So he orders something sugary and virgin that's probably actually worse for him than alcohol and turns to survey the scene.

It takes a few minutes for his eyes to adjust to the dimmer light inside the club, but once they do, Xander spots the guy almost immediately. He's not noticeably taller than anyone around him, but the white tank top he's wearing practically glows against the warm brown of his skin, showing off nicely muscled arms. The jeans he's wearing aren't bad either, hugging the curves of what looks like a very nice ass.

Either he senses Xander staring or the natural motion of the dance has him turning to look toward the bar. Whichever it is, he eyes Xander up and down in blatant appraisal before tilting his head to the side and smirking a little in invitation.

Xander drains the last of his drink and leaves the cash on the bar, never breaking eye contact. The man's smile widens as Xander approaches, full lips parting slightly to reveal a flash of white teeth.

He leans in close enough that his lips are almost brushing Xander's ear, which, to be fair, is the only way he could hope to be heard over the music. "Dance with me?"

"I'd rather take you home," Xander half-yells back.

He throws his head back in a laugh, dimples flashing under those gorgeous cheekbones. "Maybe later. Let's see your moves first, pretty boy."

Xander returns the challenging smile with one of his own, sliding his hands around the guy's waist. His thumb brushes up under the hem of the white tank top, finding warm skin as he steps in closer and starts to move. "I'm Xander," he says.

"Nick." The guy—Nick—slides his hands up Xander's back, firm and warm, moves liquidly against him.

Xander almost wishes he could step back, admire the way Nick moves, but he doesn't really want to. As good as Nick looks when he dances, he feels even better pressed up against Xander, warm and solid and real.

They get closer and closer as they dance, until their legs are slotted together. Nick's hard, muscled thigh against Xander's crotch is a tantalizing pressure, sending sparks dancing up his spine. Xander dips his head, just a little, brushes his lips over the side of Nick's neck.

Nick rewards him with a full-body shiver that turns into a roll of his hips. "Okay," he laughs. "You wanna get out of here?"

"I really do."

They cling together for a few more minutes of delicious friction, but finally Nick steps back, his hands lingering for a moment before he laces their fingers together and leads Xander off the dance floor.

XANDER'S front door is still still swinging shut behind them when Nick nudges him up against it, leaning up enough to bring their mouths together. Despite the urgency simmering between them during the ride from the club, Nick kisses unhurriedly, leisurely. His tongue slides over Xander's lips before slipping inside, making a satisfied little noise in the back of his throat when Xander opens to him.

It's amazing, but the lingering tension under Xander's skin won't let him stand still for kissing. Not when he can slide his hands under that tight tank top to find warm skin, smooth and soft under his hands. Not when he can pull, getting Nick tight against him all the way down their bodies. Not when he can roll his hips and get almost-good-enough pressure against his cock, hard and aching in his jeans.

"Impatient, huh?" Nick chuckles.

Xander arches off the wall as far as he can get as Nick kisses down his neck, the contrast between soft lips and neatly-trimmed beard lighting up all of his nerve endings. "I just—fuck, that's good." Another chuckle from Nick reminds him to drag his attention back to what he was saying. "I know what I want."

"Oh yeah?" Nick fastens his teeth lightly on Xander's neck, sucks gently. "Whaddya want, pretty boy?"

"Well..." Xander runs his hands back down Nick's back, teases them under the waistband of his jeans. "First I wanna suck you off a little."

Nick's hands flex on his hips, digging in just a little. "I think I'm down with that. Then what?"

Xander lowers his voice. "Then I want you to bend me over my bed and fuck my brains out."

"We can definitely make that happen," Nick breathes, curling his fingers in Xander's henley and tugging it up. He pauses when it's bunched under Xander's arms, leaning in for another kiss, his hands stroking over the skin he'd just bared.

When they come up for air, they're both breathing hard. Xander lets go of Nick reluctantly, lifting his arms so Nick can pull his shirt off and then returning the favor with Nick's tank top.

"Jesus, look at you." Nick's hands are everywhere, fingers tracing the lines of Xander's tattoos as they skim up his arms, sliding down his chest and making him shiver when they brush over his nipples, combing through the trail of hair leading downward.

"I'd rather look at you." Xander curls his hands around Nick's biceps, savoring the feel of them flexing under his hold before spinning them around and slipping to his knees.

At eye level, the bulge in Nick's jeans is even more impressive, enough to make Xander's mouth water. He pops the button open and pulls the zipper down one-handed, using the other hand to fish out the condom he'd stashed in his pocket earlier.

"How about that." Nick cards his fingers through Xander's hair as he leans back against the wall, his voice amused this time. "All prepared. You must've been a boy scout."

Xander smiles up at him without answering, holding the condom packet in his teeth and pulling Nick's jeans and boxer briefs down in one quick motion. Nick's cock is gorgeous, thick and hard against his thigh and cut, too. Xander wraps his hand around it, giving a couple of experimental pumps before Nick's hand tugs gently at his hair.

"Keep that up and I can't guarantee I'll last long enough to fuck you," he warns, his eyes hot and intent on Xander's face. "Not that I'm complaining."

"Of course not," Xander retorts when his mouth is free again, but he rips the condom packet open and rolls it down over Nick's cock, stroking a few more times before taking it in his mouth.

It's like stepping onto the ice, or picking up a stick. Xander loses himself in the sense of familiarity, the comfort of muscle memory settling into his bones. His own arousal is an almost distant thing compared to the high of this. Every sensation—the hot weight of a cock on his tongue, the scent of arousal in his nose, the little sounds coming from above him, even the ache of his knees against the hardwood floor—just has him flying higher.

This is what he does. He's good at this; he knows how to use his lips and tongue and the slightest hint of teeth to have Nick's hands tightening in his hair before pulling him off with an obscene slurping noise.

"Fuck," Nick gasps, dragging him to his feet. "I'm really, really not going to last. Where's your bedroom?"

"Last door on the left." Xander wraps his fingers around Nick's wrist and leads the way, suddenly impatient and aware of the way his cock is aching in his jeans.

Nick doesn't require any urging, following so closely that Xander can feel his body heat radiating across the space between them. He takes the tube Xander fishes out of his bedside drawer and tosses it onto the mattress, kissing him, deep and hungry.

"I'm feeling a little underdressed, here," he rasps when he pulls back, sliding his hands down Xander's chest to hook under the waistband of his jeans. "Let's get these off you, huh?"

Xander nods, reaching for the button, but Nick bats his hands gently away and strips him out of jeans and boxers with quick, efficient movements. Kissing is even better when they're both naked, skin on skin and the delicious friction of Nick's cock against his. Xander whines a little when Nick pulls away, but then he's being turned around, one big hand pressing between his shoulderblades until he's bent over the side of the mattress, exactly as he'd requested.

"This good?" Nick asks, brushing his lips over Xander's shoulderblade as he reaches for the discarded lube.

"Yeah," Xander breathes, crossing his arms under his head. "Yeah, this—yeah."

Nick's chuckle almost covers the sound of the lube cap opening, but not quite. "I aim to please," he quips, one hand curling around Xander's hip just before a slick fingertip skates over his entrance.

Xander grinds down against the mattress, just a little, all of his conscious attention focused on relaxing as Nick rubs teasing circles around and over his hole, never quite pressing inside. "I'm not gonna break," he growls after what feels like a torturous eternity.

"You never heard of anticipation?" Nick retorts,

but he pushes just the tip of his finger inside at the same time.

"Heard of it," Xander gasps, trying to lift his hips, get more of that long, thick finger inside him. It's been a few days since he's had time for anything other than a quick jerk-off in the shower. This is amazing, but he needs—he wants— "More, I can take it."

Nick huffs out a breath, but then there's the coolness of more lube against his skin, the stretch of a second finger sliding into his ass. It's almost over-whelming, the way it narrows his focus down to this one part of his body, the way he has to focus, to relax and take it.

"You okay?" Nick asks, pausing once he's worked his fingers as deep as they'll go.

"Fine," Xander snaps, or tries to—even to his own ears he sounds breathless, half-wrecked already. "I told you. Not gonna break."

Nick starts to move his fingers again, pulling them almost all the way out before thrusting back in. After a couple of strokes the intensity of the stretch starts to fade—until he starts scissoring them apart, stretching Xander relentlessly open. "I heard you," he murmurs, the thumb of his other hand rubbing soothing circles on Xander's hip. "Should've known you'd be a bossy bottom."

"Hey!"

Xander loses his train of thought when Nick adds a third finger, pressing his forehead to the bed and taking long, deep breaths. It's so much. So full. He remembers the weight of Nick's cock on his tongue, the stretch of his lips around the girth, and shudders all over with the anticipation. Then again when Nick curls his fingertips, grazing them deliberately over his prostate.

"Didn't say I wasn't into that." Only the slightest edge of strain in Nick's voice mars his teasing, conversational tone, but his fingertips are digging into Xander's hipbone hard enough that they might leave bruises. "What do you think, pretty boy? Think you're ready for me?"

"I've *been* ready," Xander rasps, thrusting against the bed with the next slow drag across his prostate.

Nick hums consideringly. "I don't know. I'm having fun back here. You make the best noises when I do this—"

"Fuck me," Xander demands—begs, his voice going thready. The pressure on his prostate and the friction of the sheets against his cock have him clinging to control by his fingernails. "I'm ready, come on, fuck me. *Please.*"

"Well, since you asked so nicely."

The lube clicks open again. Nick's fingers slide out, leaving Xander empty and aching, listening the slick, obscene sounds of Nick's hand on his cock. He presses the head against Xander's ass, blunt, inescapable pressure, and pushes inside in one slow, endless stroke.

"Fuck," Xander chants, the sheet bunching in his fists. It's so much. He wants to shove back, he wants to move away, but he's pinned in place by Nick's weight, Nick's hands on his hips. All he can do is take it, deeper and deeper until finally, finally Nick is pressed against him, hipbones sharp against the curve of his ass. "Fuck, fuck—"

"Still good?" Nick's voice is tense and breathless as he goes still.

Xander nods frantically, even though that's kind of a lie. It's not good. It's perfect. "I'm good. You can—you can move."

"Maybe I need a minute," Nick shoots back, bending slightly to brush his lips over Xander's shoulderblade. They both make an inarticulate noise at the way that shifts Nick's cock inside him, changing the angle, then again when Nick pushes back in that fraction of an inch he'd lost.

"Do you want me to beg?" It isn't entirely a rhetorical question; at this point, with his orgasm dangling tantalizingly just out of reach, there isn't a lot Xander wouldn't do to get there. Something about the twist in his stomach when he contemplates the idea makes him think that he might even enjoy it.

Nick pulls out and thrusts back in, just a little. "I don't know, that might be hot. Give it a shot."

"Please," Xander grits out.

"Please what?" Nick goes still again, the fucker.

Xander tries to push back, to get the movement he needs, but he has no leverage, not unless he wants to get rough enough to maybe end this right now. Which is the last thing he wants. He swallows, hard. "Please fuck me."

He gets a couple of deeper, longer thrusts for that. "Keep going," Nick orders when he falls silent.

"Please," Xander babbles, feeling his face go hot, but somehow that makes it better, the squirmy feeling in his stomach twisting together with the orgasm building at the base of his spine to make something bigger. "Please, fuck, please fuck me."

"How?" Nick demands, pulling almost all the

way out and then pushing back in, agonizingly slowly. "You want it slow and sweet? Tell me what you want, pretty boy."

Xander whimpers, fighting Nick's restraining hands, just a little. "Harder," he gasps. "Please, fuck me harder. Faster."

That gets him one hard, almost punishing stroke. "Do you like this?" Nick demands. "Me making you talk? Making you beg for it?"

"Yes," Xander admits, his voice barely audible even to himself.

Nick's hand fists in his hair, pulling his face up out of the sheet. "I can't hear you, pretty boy."

"I like it," he admits, eyes closed.

"Good," Nick praises, and fuck, that's even better. "Keep going. Let me hear you. Tell me what you want."

Xander sucks in a breath. "Please, fuck me harder, faster, please, God, yes, just like that, please—"

He loses the train of words as Nick finds a hard, perfect rhythm, nothing but little punched-out sounds falling out of his mouth. He's so close, close—

His upper body arches up off the bed when he comes, shuddering as Nick fucks him relentlessly through it. Just when he thinks it's over, Nick's cock slides over his prostate, coaxing another spurt out of his softening cock, another shivering after-shock wracking his body as Nick finally loses his rhythm, thrusting deep one last time before going still.

"Fuck," Nick gasps, collapsing down over Xander's back. His heart is pounding in his chest, beating a frenetic rhythm against Xander's skin, his breath coming in harsh gulps.

His weight feels so good, solid and grounding, that Xander can't even really mind the fact that it's pressing him down into a puddle of his own semen. He relaxes into the post-coital feeling, endorphins racing through his body, and waits for his own heart rate to slow.

Eventually Nick straightens up with a sigh, pulling carefully out. "Cool if I use your shower?"

"Yeah, sure. Towels under the sink."

"Sweet."

Xander forces himself to move up onto the bed, out of the wet spot, just in time for a really excellent view of Nick's ass as he disappears into the bath-room. The toilet flushes after a minute, water runs in the sink, and then the more distant rushing of the shower turning on.

Before too long, just as Xander is weighing the annoyance of getting up to turn off the light versus sleeping with it on, Nick reappears in the doorway, towel wrapped around his waist. "You look like you're about to pass out."

"Somebody wore me out," Xander replies with a lazy shrug, watching the leftover water droplets make their way down Nick's naked chest.

Nick returns the smirk. "Just doing what you asked, pretty boy. Do you remember where my pants ended up?"

"Hallway?" Xander guesses. "I was a little preoccupied."

"Same," Nick says lightly. "Don't get up on my account; I can show myself out."

Xander pushes himself up to sit on the side of the bed, reaching for his discarded boxers and pulling them on. "Nah, I'm good."

Nick refuses to let Xander call him a Lyft—"It's already on the way. Don't sweat it."—and leaves without a backward look.

4

JORDAN

Jordan notices it as soon as he walks into the locker room. The hickey isn't huge, but it's dark and obvious against the pale skin of Xander's trapezius.

You don't get to be jealous, he tells himself firmly, tearing his eyes away and looking somewhere, anywhere else. *You told him no.*

Logic doesn't stop the sick swirl of jealousy in the pit of his stomach. Doesn't stop him from imagining the context of it's creation, Xander's head tipped back while some faceless guy—or girl, Jordan forces himself to acknowledge—licks and bites and sucks, leaving undeniable proof of their existence behind. Sure, Xander always kicks his bedmates out and never goes back for seconds, but for at least one night, they got to have him.

It was the right decision. You don't want the same things.

It's all true.

None of it helps.

The only good thing about Xander's hookup is that it seems to have cleared out the awkwardness between them. But Jordan's not entirely sure that's a benefit. He knows that Xander flirts with everyone. He knows this. It's part of why he said no in the first place.

But knowing something in the abstract is different than having to deal with the concrete reality. With Xander languidly stripping his shirt off as he walks into the trainers room, every movement an exercise in seduction. He seems to have made it his mission in life to sound like he's having an orgasm every time he comes in for a shoulder massage, moaning and groaning fit to make a porn star jealous.

But the worst, the absolute worst, is the touching.

Xander's always been tactile, even for a hockey player, but he seems to have dialed it up to 11.

Jordan spends the entire day mentally cataloging all the places Xander touches him. It's all perfectly innocent, a brush of fingers over Jordan's bicep to get his attention, an offered fist bump he can't turn down, a slap on the back that maybe possibly lingers a second longer than it has to.

He hates it.

Except that he doesn't.

Except he feels like a teenager again, mooning over the slightest interaction and picking it apart, looking for significance. It's ridiculous. He's twenty-seven goddamn years old. Too old for this shit.

Too bad nobody told his heart.

Jordan was wrong. The *actual* worst part is that Xander needs a massage every day. Legitimately needs, for his athletic performance. So Jordan has to suck it up, be a professional, and do his fucking job. Which involves putting his hands all over the incredibly attractive, half-naked professional athlete he has a stupid crush on.

Fuck. His. Life.

On Sunday, Xander is already shirtless when he comes through the door, so Jordan gets an eyeful of flexing muscles under tattooed skin and rippling abs. All of this before Xander sits down.

Jordan takes a deep breath, summoning all of his self-control. Probably the most unfair thing about all of this is that he never seems to get desensitized to this, to his hands on Xander's skin. Every time is just as bad as the first, if not worse. It should be illegal for anything to feel as good as the texture of Xander's chest and back and shoulder under Jordan's palms.

"Fuck, that's good," Xander groans into the table, practically writhing when Jordan's fingers dig into a particularly tense spot. "Yeah, right there. Harder."

Somehow Jordan manages to keep his hands going while all the blood in his body does it's best to flow into his stupid, ignorant cock. He thinks frantically about bloody noses, the stink of day-old protein shaker bottles, anything to keep him from embarrassing himself. Xander doesn't make it easy, a string of porn-style moans and groans and dialogue that makes Jordan seriously question whether or not he's doing it on purpose.

The only saving grace is that Xander is face-down for most of the massage, so he has no idea how dumb Jordan is being right now. There's no one else in the trainers room, so Jordan can keep the table between them until Xander's gone. Can slip into the single-occupancy staff restroom and lock the door, hands shaking.

His reflection in the mirror above the sink looks back at him like everything is normal. Like it's just another day. Like his cock isn't hard and aching in his pants.

He turns away from the mirror when he palms it, sucking in a breath at how good it feels, even through the muffling layers of cloth. Doing his best to ignore the tiny, guilty voice in his head, he frees his erection, wrapping his hand around it and stroking.

It's so good, that first slightly too-dry slide of skin on skin. It feels like he's been hard for hours, balancing on that torturous edge. He does his best not to think of anyone in particular, but that battle was lost before it started. The image of Xander is burned behind his eyelids, flexing muscles and dark ink against paler skin. Xander's voice echoes in his ears, the fantasy so close to the reality that Jordan can almost taste it.

"Right there," Xander moans, holding onto the

table as Jordan fucks into him. "Just like that, baby. Harder."

Jordan shifts enough to get a hand around Xander's cock. "You feel so good, don't know how long I'm gonna last. Gonna come for me, babe?"

"Yeah," Xander pants, pushing back into Jordan's thrusts. "So close, baby, so good. Fuck, right there—"

Jordan bites his lip as he comes, trying desperately to stay quiet. He slumps against the sink for a minute, catching his breath and waiting until his heart rate has slowed down to something like normal before cleaning up his mess and washing his hands.

Within a few minutes, he's back in the trainers room looking, to all outward appearances, like nothing has happened. Like he wasn't just so worked up by doing his fucking job that he had to go jerk off in the bathroom like a teenager.

Something has to change. Something has to give. The season hasn't even started yet; another thirty weeks of this might actually kill him.

THE GUY STANDS as Jordan approaches the table. "Hi," he says, offering his hand. "I'm Chris."

"Jordan."

They shake, hands lingering a little, and take their seats. Chris is, honestly, even more attractive in person than in his Tinder profile, blue eyes behind dark-framed glasses picking up the shade of his button-down shirt. His sleeves are rolled up, exposing muscular forearms with just a hint of a tattoo peeking out from under the fabric.

Jordan would feel worse about the once-over if Chris wasn't doing the same assessment. Their waitress arrives before the moment can become awkward, getting their drink order before vanishing again.

"Thanks for coming out on such a weird night," Jordan says for something to break the silence.

"Yeah, no problem." Chris smiles at him. "I guess it's hard, huh, with the games and having to be there on weekends?"

Jordan shrugs. "I don't usually think about it anymore, unless it comes to things like dating. But it throws a lot of people with 'normal' jobs off. What did you say you do, again?"

"I'm in human resources." Chris waves a dismissive hand. "It's not as glamorous as professional sports, but it pays the bills."

Applying the word "glamorous" to the CHL has Jordan snickering. "Glamorous. Right."

Chris grins in answer, more real than the slightly practiced smile of before. "What, it's not all red carpets and black tie galas?"

"That's for the team," Jordan retorts. "I get to deal with torn ligaments, broken teeth, and every kind of bruising under the sun. Not to mention giant man-children who think they're immortal and invincible until they learn the hard way that they aren't."

"Okay, but the eye candy is pretty nice. I've seen that charity calendar."

Jordan nods a little weakly. Everyone's seen the charity calendar; every year they do a photo shoot before PR selects twelve glossy, high-resolution photos of various members of the team for inclusion. Last year's theme had been "Go Wild," and their genius photographer had decided that mostly naked hockey players in nature was clearly the best way to accomplish that brief.

It sold like hotcakes, of course, having to be reprinted three times. And a big part of the demand had been leaked photos from the shoot of one Xander Richards, coming up out of a lake like a Bond girl walking out of the ocean.

Jordan wrenches his mind forcibly back on track. This date is supposed to be about moving on, getting past his stupid crush, not fixating on mental images of Xander. "Yeah, well. There's only so many smelly jockstraps and terrible jokes you can take before even the best eye candy loses its appeal."

Chris doesn't look convinced. Which is fair, because Jordan is lying through his fucking teeth. Even the most disgusting habits haven't been enough to kill his infatuation with Xander; not that he has that many—whatever.

Fortunately their appetizers arrive in that moment, distracting them from the conversational lull. "So," Chris says, scooping some of the bruschetta onto a piece of toast. "Did you finish that book yet?"

Conversation flows pretty naturally for the rest of the meal. After they discuss the book Jordan had just finished, they segue into other books they've both read and liked, with a little playful wrangling when Jordan discovers that Chris has never read Terry Pratchett. That leads to movies and that leads to TV shows and before Jordan knows it, they're sitting there, dishes long since cleared away and the waitstaff politely and pointedly coming to check if they need anything else.

"I guess we should get out of here and let them have the table," he says, pushing his chair back reluctantly.

"Probably," Chris agrees, standing.

They both hesitate once they're outside the restaurant door, looking at each other.

"Do you—"

"Would you—"

They laugh, stuttering to a halt as they talk over each other. Chris throws his head back a little when he laughs, Jordan notices.

"Anyway," Chris chuckles. "Do you want to take a walk or something? It's a nice night."

Jordan smiles back at him. "Sure, sounds good."

It really is a beautiful night, cooled down now from the heat of the day, the sky darkening to indigo. They cross the street and take one of the paths through the little park there, meandering aimlessly under the trees as they talk.

When Chris's hand lands on his arm, Jordan lets himself be pulled closer, too far inside Chris's personal space for either of them to mistake what is happening.

"Is this okay?" Chris asks, sliding that hand slowly up to Jordan's shoulder and leaning in even further.

"Yeah," Jordan breathes, bending down enough to meet him halfway.

The kiss is soft and a little tentative, just a quiet press of lips at first. Jordan steps in closer, sliding a hand around Chris's waist and pressing their bodies together. Chris's lips part under his and he takes the invitation, deepening the kiss.

When they finally separate, the expression on Chris's face matches the one Jordan can feel on his own.

"That was nice," Chris says.

Jordan nods. It was nice. But—

"But I think we both deserve more than just nice," Chris continues, his eyes determined and kind. "You're a great guy and you're super hot."

"You too," Jordan blurts out, stepping back. "But—yeah."

Chris smiles, wry and self-deprecating. "Look, you've got my number. If you ever want to hang out or catch a movie or something, that'd be cool. I just moved to Milwaukee a few months ago; I can use all the friends I can get."

"I don't actually have that many friends I don't work with," Jordan admits, stuffing his hands in his pockets. "Sounds good."

It's surprisingly comfortable as they make their

way back to where they'd parked. "It's a shame," Chris says mildly, pausing next to Jordan's car. "We would've made a hot couple."

Jordan laughs. "Yeah, we would have. If you ever need a wingman or a kissing reference, just let me know."

"Same." Chris offers his hand, pulls Jordan in for a hug. "Maybe I'll catch a game sometime. See if I can figure out which of those hockey players gets you so flustered."

"I—you—" Jordan splutters, but stops trying to deny it when Chris gives him a knowing look. "Yeah, okay. I can get you tickets, if you want."

Chris starts walking backwards down the sidewalk. "I'll hold you to that."

Jordan makes his way home on autopilot, doing his best not to think about anything. Not about failing spectacularly in his attempts to forget about Xander and move on. Not about the fact that his crush is so obvious that even a near-complete stranger can see it. Not about going in to work tomorrow and attempt to do his job when nothing has changed.

The buzzing of his phone in the cup holder pulls him out of his reverie. He hits the button to answer the call. "Hello?"

"Oh, so you can answer the phone but you can't take two minutes to call your grandmother?"

"Hi, Nana," he sighs. "What's up?"

She laughs. "I need a reason to call my favorite grandson?"

"I'm your only grandson," he points out.

"Which means you're also my least favorite. Are you in your car? Why are you talking on your phone while you're driving?"

Jordan rolls his eyes. "I'm on speaker, eyes on the road, both hands on the wheel. Which is it, Nana? Gonna chew me out for talking to you? Or for not talking to you?"

"Don't sass me, boy." The creak of the porch swing carries over the phone. He can almost see it, Nana rocking gently back and forth on the porch in the evening light, fanning herself with one of those cardboard church fans. "Where are you drivin' to this late at night?"

He briefly considers lying, but somehow she always knows. "On my way home from a date."

"Oh really?" Nana says, elaborately casual. "And?"

"And he's a very nice guy, maybe a friend, but there's not really anything else there." Jordan sighs, suddenly feeling exhausted. "Nothing else to tell, really."

She hums softly, the swing creaking in the background. "Don't worry, honey. When it's time, it'll happen."

"Aren't you the one who's always telling me the Lord helps those who help themselves?"

He can picture Nana's eyes narrowing as she clicks her tongue. "It sounds like you're doing all you can to help yourself right now, aren't you?"

"Yeah, I guess."

"Then that's all you can do." Her voice softens. "I'm proud of you, Jordan. I wish you could've gotten a job with the Saints or somebody not all the way up north, but you're doing good work."

Jordan clears his throat. "Thanks, Nana."

"Now you'd better hang up and pay attention to your driving. And call me once in awhile!"

"I will, promise. Love you, Nana."

The smile in her voice is as clear as day. "I love you too, honey."

Jordan drives the rest of the way home in silence, parking in the garage and scanning his key fob absently to call the elevator. Thankfully it's empty when it finally comes, so he doesn't have to make small talk with any of his neighbors on the way up

Locking his his apartment door behind him, he strips off his clothes on the way to bed, not bothering to turn out the lights. Despite how tired he feels, it takes hours for him to fall asleep that night.

5

XANDER

Xander carefully balances the two coffees as he heads toward the arena entrance. Fortunately Zubeck gets there just before him and holds the door. Even more fortunately, Zubeck is the kind of guy who doesn't comment if he notices something weird. Like, for example, Xander bringing in two coffee cups instead of just one. Or Xander heading for the trainers room instead of turning toward the locker room to get dressed for practice.

His lucky streak continues when he finds Jordan alone in the trainers room, finishing up some paperwork. So engrossed, in fact, that he doesn't even notice Xander come in.

"Hey," he says after deciding against an awkward throat-clearing.

Jordan's head shoots up and he twists around in his chair. "Uh, hey. What's up? Shoulder bothering you?"

Xander shakes his head, offering the extra coffee. "No, I, uh—I thought you might like a coffee? Kind of a thank-you for all the time you're putting in on me."

"It's my job," Jordan protests, but he does take the coffee cup, so Xander counts that as a victory.

The silence stretches then, awkward and just a little uncomfortable, and Xander finds himself blurting out the question he'd promised himself he wouldn't ask. "Look, man. No pressure, totally legit that you didn't want to go out. Just wondered if I could—ask why?"

Jordan's eyes are unusually serious when he meets Xander's. "Because this is my job, and we both have to work here. One night in bed with you isn't worth how awkward it would be after."

"Are you sure?" Xander asks, flirting reflexively.

"You don't know me." Jordan says, clearly restraining the urge to roll his eyes. "You saw someone who looks like your type—"

"My type is everyone."

Jordan does roll his eyes at that. "Uh, yeah. Anybody who's worked with you knows that. Whatever. The point is, you don't actually want me, because you don't know me. You want my body, and I've had enough of that to last me a lifetime. I don't just want a fuck, even a truly spectacular fuck. I'm ready for a relationship. And you—" he pins Xander with a dismissive look "—you aren't."

He unfolds himself from his chair and bypasses Xander, heading out the door with his coffee, while Xander is still trying to process what happened.

XANDER FINALLY SHAKES himself out of his reverie when Marian comes into the trainers room, tsks at him, and physically pushes him toward the door. He's one of the last into the locker room, stripping down and putting on his gear mechanically, his mind whirring. He replays the conversation over and over, trying to figure out where things went sideways.

The coffee was probably fine, he decides as he pulls on his compression gear. Jordan took it, drank it, so that wasn't the problem. And so what if he's attracted to Jordan on a physical level? Is that a fucking crime now? It's not like he's the only one. Now that he's looking, he's seen the way Jordan looks at him, and maybe, just maybe, he's been showing off a little bit. Jordan is attracted to him, too. He'd take bets on it. So what's the big fucking deal?

He straps on his pads and pulls his socks, pants, and practice jersey over the top, silently fuming. Where the fuck does Jordan Darling get off, anyway? What business is it of his how Xander chooses to live his life? So what if he can't remember the last time he's seen the same person twice? Some people just aren't built for relationships. Should he pretend otherwise? Trick some poor guy or girl into what they think is a monogamous relationship and then fuck them over by cheating on them at every turn? Fake being in love with them until they see through it and leave him?

The anger carries him through practice, giving him a little extra edge, but it leaves him drained by the end of it, even more tired than usual. He stands in the showers, scrubbing himself off perfunctorily and trying to convince himself that the aching throb in his shoulder feels better, that there's no need to visit the trainers room.

He's never been very good at lying to himself.

He dries off reluctantly, pulling on his t-shirt and shorts like things will change if he just delays. Like another massage therapist will just fucking drop out of the sky and start working for the team. Finally, though, he can't procrastinate any longer, and he makes his way down to the trainers room, dreading the awkwardness that he can already feel.

Except it's not actually that awkward, is the thing. Erikssen is on one of the tables when he comes in, his face a particularly ridiculous cross between agony and relief. Jordan nods at Xander, jerking his head toward the other table, and Xander pulls out his phone to keep himself occupied with something other than watching Jordan.

It doesn't really work, though. He keeps getting caught by the movement in the corner of his eye and looking up before he realizes it. His phone keeps going to sleep and having to be unlocked again because he gets lost watching Jordan move. By the time Erikssen makes his way out of the trainers room, leaving them alone, he's still at the top of his Twitter feed and there are 132 new tweets on his timeline.

At this point they don't really need to talk much about his shoulder; it is what it is and Jordan probably knows what's wrong with it better than

Xander does. Xander shucks off his shirt, looking determinedly at a point on the wall as Jordan steps in and starts to massage away the tightness and the soreness.

As much as he'd like to remain stoically silent, he can't keep the little grunts and groans from escaping his mouth as Jordan works the tension out of his muscles. It's not like he didn't know how sexual they sounded before; he wasn't above playing it up a little to try and make Jordan realize what he was missing. By the time Jordan finishes, Xander's face is burning, and he slips out of the trainers room with a muttered "thanks" and his metaphorical tail between his legs.

XANDER ALMOST DOESN'T ANSWER the Skype call, but he knows if he doesn't he's going to have Justin *and* Brooke texting and calling him to be sure he's okay. He wouldn't put it past Justin to actually bully one of the other guys on the team into coming over to his apartment to check on him. So he hits the button to accept and does his best to put on a normal expression.

"Who pissed in your beer?" is Justin's opening line, so it seems like he didn't succeed.

"Nobody—nothing." He does his best to brush it off. "Just tired. Long practice, shoulder's sore. You know."

Justin eyes him closely. "Nope. Nice try, but you should know better than to try and lie to me. C'mon, Xan. Spill."

"It's dumb."

"Since when has that fucking stopped you? What, was your last pickup bad in bed or something?"

Xander sighs. "No."

"Look, if you don't talk to me, I'm gonna go get Brooke. And you know you're gonna end up telling her. Make it easy on yourself," Justin coaxes.

"Fine, you asked for it." Xander takes a minute, tries to line the words up in a way that makes sense, but he takes so long that Justin starts to get up off of the couch. "Ugh, okay. You remember Jordan, the trainer?"

Justin nods, sinking back down. "Darling, yeah. Does the training and the massage therapy. Nice guy—oh, fuck. Xan, tell me you didn't fuck him. That's so fucking stupid, bro."

"No, I didn't," Xander retorts.

"Good." Justin eyeballs him. "But, what? You want to? Look, I know he's hot as hell, but that is not a good idea."

"I know!" Xander throws up his hands. "Anyway, he shot me down."

Justin bursts into laughter, his face screwed up like a little kid. Tears stream from the corners of his eyes, and every time he starts to catch his breath, he takes a look at Xander and starts up again. He laughs for long enough that Brooke appears on the screen, clearly drawn by the sound from whatever part of their house she was in.

"Xander, did you break my husband?" she asks, looking from Justin to the screen in front of him.

"Not on purpose, but you know how delicate he is," Xander chirps.

Brooke rolls her eyes. "Boy, do I ever. Do I even want to know?"

"I have no idea," Xander says honestly.

"You do," Justin wheezes between laughs, his voice breaking. "You really do."

She settles down next to Justin on the couch, far enough away that she won't get nailed by any flailing limbs, because she's a smart lady. "All right, Richards. Spill."

It's Xander's turn to roll his eyes. "You know,

that's almost exactly what he said. You two are turning into one of those disgusting married couples that talk like each other."

"Yeah, yeah, quit stalling and dish," Brooke says.

"Fine. I don't know if you remember Jordan?"

She nods. "The massage guy? Wait, did you fuck him? What were you thinking!"

"Jesus, you guys are supposed to be my friends," Xander groans.

"Honey, we are your friends. And friends tell you when you're doing stupid shit."

He flops back onto the couch, almost losing his grip on the phone for a second. "Well, I didn't sleep with him. I asked him out and he shot me down."

Brooke stares at him for a moment, then starts laughing, which sets Justin off again.

Xander props the phone up against the couch cushions and waits for them to calm down. After a few minutes, he starts humming the Final Jeopardy theme.

"Sorry," Brooke says finally, wiping her eyes. "But you have to admit, it's funny."

"If you say so," Xander mutters.

She sighs. "Okay, but seriously. I'm sure you've been turned down before, even if I can't remember it happening. Aren't you the one who's always like 'there's plenty of fish in the sea'? Did this just happen today?"

He shakes his head. "Last week. But I asked him today why."

"And he said—?"

"He said I didn't know him. That he wants a relationship, not just a one-night thing. And that I don't."

Brooke purses her lips. "And that makes you feel—what?"

Xander bites down the surge of irritation rising in his chest. "I don't know."

She turns to Justin. "Honey, could you give us a minute?"

"As long as you promise not to run away to Milwaukee and leave me for Xander," he says easily, kissing her cheek before getting to his feet.

"Only if you keep leaving your socks on the floor," she retorts. "Why don't you take Vivi out, walk her around the block."

He salutes lazily, waves at Xander, and ambles out of the frame. Eager barking sounds in the background, and then a door opening and shutting.

"Okay," Brooke says. "Does this have something to do with your feelings for Justin?"

Xander's face flames hot, panic shooting electric down his spine. "I—you—what—"

She doesn't look mad, he realizes. Her smile is soft and a little sad. "For what it's worth, I don't think he knows. You hide it pretty well. I think the only reason I noticed is sometimes you look at him the same way I do."

"Fuck." Xander scrubs his free hand over his face. "I'm sorry."

"Nothing to be sorry for," she says. "Unless you're planning on trying to steal him from me. Then we might have words."

He shakes his head vehemently. "No, I—no."

"Kidding, honey. But you still haven't answered my question."

It takes a minute, and a couple of deep breaths, to slow his racing heart, to focus on what she'd asked. "I—I don't know. Maybe it's just that I have to see him every day? But, I don't know. It's just weird, with you two in Seattle. I keep going to tell Justin something or text you about something we should do, and then I remember."

Brooke nods. "Yeah. It's been hard for us, too."

They sit in silence for a minute. Xander feels something inside of him relax, something he hadn't even realized was tense.

"Look," she finally says. "You and Justin have always been close. It's not like you weren't friendly with other guys on the team, but not the same way. But we're not there anymore. You're going to have to put on your big boy pants and learn how to make friends."

He groans. "That sounds terrible."

"Nobody's going to make you," she says, her voice entirely reasonable. "But don't come crying to me when you're sitting all alone in that big fucking house because you have nobody to hang out with."

"Ugh, fine."

Brooke grins at him. "You know I'm right. You can start with Jordan." She holds up a silencing hand when Xander starts to speak. "Not because that might help you get into his pants, because I can almost guarantee you it won't. But he already kind of knows you, and he's not going to go all starstruck on you. Besides. It'll make you seem like less of an asshole."

"I hate it when you're right," Xander grumbles.

"I know."

6

JORDAN

Their first regular season game is at home versus the Jackalopes. It's a tense first two periods, the Jacks matching them goal for goal. But something, maybe David's earnest speech in the locker room, lights a fire under the Wendigos in the third. Harty scores on his first shot of the period, off an absolutely filthy pass from Sasha that has the entire bench, including Jordan, on their feet, screaming themselves hoarse. They manage to hold the score until the last minute of the period, when Xander scores another goal, and the arena erupts.

The whole team is high on the win, jostling and wrestling in the locker room. It's contagious, and Jordan has to keep reminding himself that there are still eighty-one games left in the season, that this is only the beginning of the long road ahead.

They pile out of the arena and into JP's, the team and the staff all coming together. The married guys beg off after one celebratory drink, heading home to their families, and Jordan has never been so keenly aware of the fact that he's the only one on the training staff without a spouse, the table full of people emptying until it's just him, toying with his half-full beer bottle. He's trying to decide which would be more pathetic, gulping it down and slipping out, or trying to insert himself into one of the other tables, when someone pulls out the chair across from him.

And of fucking course it's Xander, because why wouldn't it be? His hair is still damp from the shower, roughly finger-combed back with a couple of strands falling over his forehead, his cheeks still faintly pink from the exertion of the evening. It's just one more unfairness on top of Jordan's already sour mood, making him unusually blunt.

"If you're here to ask me out again, you can just move the fuck along."

"I'm here to say you're right," Xander says, looking down at his hands, wrapped around his glass.

Jordan gapes at him for a minute before he realizes and closes his mouth. He glances around, but nobody seems to have noticed, too busy with replaying the game—David, Mac, and Sasha have their heads together as usual—or stuffing their faces or, in the case of King and McDaniel, trying to figure out how to talk to women.

"Okay," he says cautiously.

Xander looks up at him. "Look, I'm not—I don't have to justify my love life to anybody. I don't —I've only felt like I wanted more than sex with one person, and they didn't feel the same. I don't know if I *can* feel that way about anybody else. But it was a dick move to keep pushing you, and I'm sorry."

Jordan blinks at him for a second. "I—thanks. Apology accepted."

"Cool." Xander actually looks relieved, which kind of blows Jordan's mind. "It's been weird, with Justin gone. Brooke—I don't know if you remember Brooke?"

"Yeah, of course."

One corner of Xander's mouth quirks up. "She thinks I need to try and make more friends here. Since she and Justin are in fucking Seattle. Can— can we forget all this shit and start over?"

Jordan nods, mostly because he's not sure what else to do. This whole conversation has just been surreal. "Uh, yeah?"

"Cool." Xander reaches across the table, offering his hand, waiting until Jordan automatically takes it to shake. "Hi, I'm Xander. I'm kind of an asshole sometimes and definitely a slut most of the time. Nice to meet you."

"I—" Jordan gapes at him for a minute before remembering to retrieve his hand. Apparently they're doing this, even though it's kind of weird. Fortunately no one else seems to notice. "I'm Jordan. I, uh, I'm a trainer and massage therapist for the team."

Xander takes a drink of his beer. "That's pretty cool. You must be really smart, getting the training and degrees to do both of those."

Jordan's face heats and he thanks whatever deities are listening that there's know way for Xander to know that. "It was a lot of work sometimes, but I like what I do."

"So what do you do when you're not at work?" Xander asks. Everything about him, his eyes, his face, his body language, projects sincere interest.

It's kind of freaking Jordan out. It's definitely making him stumble over his words. "I, uh, nothing, really. I watch stuff on Netflix. I read, when I get a chance."

"Oh yeah?" Xander is clearly wasted on a hockey career; he should be an actor, if he can seem this interested in Jordan. "What kind of stuff do you read?"

"Scifi and fantasy, mostly," Jordan admits reluctantly, still trying to find the trap. "When I can find stuff that isn't racist as hell, anyway."

Xander winces. "Yeah, I can see that being a problem. Wasn't that part of the whole thing with the Hugos a couple of years ago? The puppies or whatever?"

"Ugh," Jordan groans. "Don't fucking remind me. Yeah. They were all 'the establishment only nominates progressive stuff instead of the really popular books.' Which is clearly code for 'I'm a racist, sexist, homophobic dickbag who wants to go back to the good old days where a white straight dude could do whatever the fuck he wants.'"

"That's bullshit," Xander says. "But if you're still reading, I'm guessing there's still some good stuff out there? What are you reading now?"

Jordan hesitates, but Xander just waits, like he has literally no other priority than to spend time with Jordan. *Friends,* Jordan reminds himself viciously. *He wants a friend.*

"I just finished binging through basically everything N.K. Jemisin has ever written," he admits. "I'm thinking about maybe doing a Pratchett reread, though. I've been putting off reading the last one, because—"

"—because if you finish it, then it's the last one," Xander finishes. "Yeah, I cried like a fucking baby when I read it."

Jordan thinks vaguely that by now he should be used to this sensation of the world tilting under his feet as his expectations rearrange themselves, but all he can do is stare blankly at Xander for a moment. "You, uh, you like Pratchett?"

"My sisters all loved him," Xander says easily, taking another drink. "They got me hooked as soon as they thought I could understand the books. I seriously lost it when he died."

"Yeah."

They sit in silence for a moment. Jordan ends up draining his beer just to have something to do with his hands and his mouth. Eventually, though, Xander appears to shake himself out of his reverie. "So, you said N.K. Jemisin? I keep hearing about her, so I'm guessing she's good."

"She's fucking amazing," Jordan says, grateful for the subject change. "Just—I can't really explain, because that would involve spoilers for like, all the books. But seriously. Just—if you like scifi or fantasy at all, you'll probably like them."

"I'll have to check them out," Xander says. "I've been reading a lot of YA books lately. I get kinda mad sometimes, like, where was this when I was a kid? But there's so much good stuff out there."

Jordan has no idea why he's so surprised that Xander admitted to reading books for teens, but he thinks the only thing that could have shocked him more would be if he'd professed his love for bodice-ripping romance novels. "I know, right? Kids today."

"No idea how good they have it," Xander agrees. "Have you read any of Timothy Zahn's stuff?"

The conversation just flows, while they each nurse another beer. Jordan is surprised to see, when he looks up after draining his second longneck, that the team has mostly cleared out.

"How late is it?" he asks, pulling out his phone and wincing at the answer. Sure, practice isn't until eleven, but since he hit thirty, getting by on less than eight hours of sleep has gotten harder and harder. "Shit. I need to get home and in bed."

Something flashes in Xander's eyes, but all he says is, "yeah, me too," as he pushes his chair back, digging out his wallet and leaving a couple of twenties on the table.

"I can—"

Xander stops him with an upraised hand. "Look, I know you guys get paid a lot, but I also know I get paid more. It's not a problem. But if it really bothers you, you can get the next one."

Jordan hesitates, torn between the impulse to insist on paying for himself and the desire not to shatter the fragile peace they'd managed to cobble together. "Fine," he says finally. "I'll get the next one."

"Deal." Xander claps him on the shoulder. "See you at practice tomorrow?"

"Same bat time, same bat channel," Jordan agrees automatically, grinning despite himself when it makes Xander burst into laughter.

"You're such a nerd," Xander says, an almost fond note in his voice.

Jordan forces that thought out of his head. "Takes one to know one."

"Yeah, yeah. See you in the morning, Batman."

"So a little birdie told me that you and Richards closed down the bar the other night," Marian says as soon as Jordan steps in the door the next morning.

"Good morning, Marian," Jordan replies, hanging his jacket over his desk chair. "I slept okay, how about you?"

She rolls her eyes. "Quit stalling, Jordy. Spill."

"Nothing to tell," he says, completely ignoring how much he wishes her assumption was correct. "I guess he's lonely with Justin in Seattle? He said Brooke told him to make new friends."

"Mmmhmm," she hums, her voice dripping with skepticism. "Friends."

Jordan sighs. "I swear. Nothing happened."

She eyes him closely for a minute longer, then turns away, apparently satisfied. "All right, then."

"Not that it would be any of your business if it did," he calls after her as she disappears into the equipment room.

"Keep telling yourself that," she yells back.

He sighs and sits down at his desk. Maybe he has enough time to get caught up on email before practice starts.

His phone vibrates in his pocket when he's halfway through his inbox. He pulls it out to see a group text from Cammie. *Game night Tuesday @6 BYOB+snacks*

Sounds good, he texts back. *Board or card*

bring both and see what happens, she replies almost instantly

He sends a thumbs-up and gets back to work. Something about knowing he gets to see his friends soon has him smiling as he deletes, replies, and forwards emails. He's so focused on his task and the dwindling number of unread messages that he doesn't even realize he's not alone until a disposable coffee cup lands on the desk next to his computer.

It's Xander, of course. Somehow Jordan doesn't even find his presence that surprising anymore. What is surprising, though, is how wrecked Xander looks. His eyes are actually closed as he sips his own coffee, the skin under them dark and bruised-looking.

"What happened to you?" Jordan blurts out.

Xander groans, opening his eyes. "I went home and ordered all of N.K. Jemisin's books and I was just going to read the first chapter—"

Jordan starts laughing; he knows he probably

shouldn't, but it's too funny. Especially when Xander breaks off to glare at him.

"Fine, laugh it up," Xander says haughtily. "But I want you to know this is all your fault."

"Hey," Jordan gasps, trying to catch his breath. "Isn't that what friends are for?"

Xander shakes his head. "I'm regretting all of my choices right now."

"I didn't come to your place and force you to start reading," Jordan points out, but he can't muster up much heat. "Which one did you start with?"

"*The Hundred Thousand Kingdoms,*" Xander mutters, draining his cup and looking at it despairingly when no more coffee is forthcoming. "It's so fucking good."

Jordan nods. "I know. Come on, you'd better get in there and start suiting up. Make it through practice and I'll let you nap on one of the tables after we take care of your shoulder."

"I'm holding you to that," Xander says darkly, but he drops his empty cup into the trash and meanders out in the general direction of the locker room.

7

———

XANDER

Xander comes home from the bar in honestly the best mood he can remember in awhile. It's kind of ridiculous, to be honest, considering he didn't even come close to getting laid. But it was actually nice to just talk to someone without any ulterior motives. For the first time since Justin got traded, he actually enjoyed himself on a team outing instead of hovering on the fringes or making an excuse to leave.

He pulls out his phone and texts Brooke. *you were right*

For a second he worries that it's too late for texting, but then he remembers the time difference. Besides, the Selkies won their game tonight, too, so she's probably out celebrating with Justin and his new team. There's still a little pang at the thought, but not as bad as it once was.

Sure enough, her response is almost instantaneous. *I usually am. What am I right about this time? there's so many things*

He sends back three eye-roll emojis before relenting. *making friends*

good 4 you, she says. *Did you actually talk to hot massage guy? or someone else?*

he has a name. Xander blinks for a second, wondering where that protective impulse came from. *but yes. we actually like some of the same books. and he recommended some others*

Fortunately, Brooke gets distracted by the later messages and doesn't latch onto Xander's instinctive defense. *Cool. I'm glad. Now go to bed!*

i'm an adult

He can practically hear her blowing a derisive raspberry at that, even before the emoji comes through. *whatever you say, honey. I'm gonna go tell Justin he's been replaced*

fine, he sends back, smiling despite himself

fine

Xander's phone is already in his hand, so he flips to the Kindle store as he walks toward his bedroom. Might as well go ahead and load up on the books Jordan recommended so he can start on them when he has a spare moment.

The covers are gorgeous, even on the small screen of his phone. By the time he's settled in bed, he doesn't really feel tired, so he opens the Kindle app. *Just one chapter and then I'll go to sleep.*

Two hours later, he swears when he checks the time. He should go to sleep, but—the app says he's got about 40 minutes left, and it's an optional skate tomorrow—

Even as he's debating with himself, his eyes have come back to the words on the screen, his thumb automatically swiping to the next page.

XANDER GROANS when the sound of his alarm finally penetrates his awareness, dragging him to consciousness. His eyes feel heavy and gritty. It takes every bit of willpower he's learned in his hockey career to force himself out of bed and into the shower, leaning against the tiled wall under the spray until his brain comes online.

By some miracle he manages to get dressed and in his car in time to hit the drive-through for second coffee on his way to the arena, since first coffee did almost nothing to wake him up. He doesn't realize until he's driving away that he'd automatically ordered Jordan a coffee as well, but he's not awake enough to really parse the implications of that.

He makes his way into the arena and to the trainers room on autopilot, where Jordan is hunched over his computer. He looks up when Xander sets his coffee down on the desk, his eyes going wide. "What happened to you?"

Xander forces his eyes open on a groan that's only a little bit for effect. "I went home and ordered all of N.K. Jemisin's books and I was just going to read the first chapter—"

He breaks off when Jordan starts laughing, vaguely annoyed under the muffling effect of tiredness. "Fine, laugh it up. But I want you to know this is all your fault."

It takes a few seconds before Jordan can stop laughing enough to speak. "Hey, isn't that what friends are for?"

Xander does his best to ignore the warmth welling up in his chest at those words. "I'm regretting all of my choices right now," he lies, shaking his head.

"I didn't come to your place and force you to start reading," Jordan points out, his words only interrupted by the occasional chuckle. "Which one did you start with?"

Xander drinks the last of his coffee—how is it gone already? "*The Hundred Thousand Kingdoms*. It's so fucking good."

"I know," Jordan agrees with a nod. "Come on, you'd better get started suiting up. Make it through practice and I'll let you nap on one of the tables after we take care of your shoulder."

"I'm holding you to that," Xander says, pretending that he's not pathetically grateful for the offer. He forces himself into motion, dropping the empty cup of betrayal into the trash can and turning to make his way toward the locker room.

JORDAN LIFTS his hands away from Xander's shoulder, the sudden rush of cooler air against his skin pulling him out of his half-doze. "Do you want your shirt back on before you take a nap? Or I have a blanket."

"Blanket, please," Xander mumbles, not bothering to open his eyes. A drawer opens and shuts somewhere in the room and then a soft, plush fabric settles over him.

"I think you're the last one, but if anybody else shows up, I can't guarantee how quiet they'll be," Jordan says, his voice hushed.

Xander just shrugs, already too far into sleep to manage words. He drifts away to the sound of Jordan's keyboard clicking quietly in the background.

WHEN XANDER WAKES UP, he's alone in the trainers room, Jordan nowhere to be found. It takes a few minutes for him to work up the will to sit up and leave the warmth of the blanket, but finally he ventures out in search of his shirt. There's still no sign of Jordan by the time he's dressed, and unfortunately no real reason for Xander to go looking for him. He folds the blanket neatly and leaves it on top of Jordan's desk. Hesitating for a moment, he grabs a scrap of paper and scribbles "Thanks" on it with, after a longer hesitation, his phone number underneath.

He second-guesses himself all the way home, but the only thing more humiliating that Jordan misinterpreting it would be Jordan catching him sneaking in to steal the note, so there's not much he can do about it right now. He does his best to put it out of his mind as he goes about his evening, heating one of the prepared meals from his freezer and settling on the couch with his plate and his phone.

The second book in the series works its magic quickly, but he still twitches every time his notifications go off, irrationally disappointed when it's Justin sending him a terrible pun or his mom wanting to know what he wants for his birthday.

He's just about convinced himself that Jordan never found the note, or that he found it and tossed it in the trash, or that he was insulted because he thought Xander was hitting on him again, when he receives a text from an unfamiliar number.

You know, technically I already have your number from the team roster, is followed a few seconds later by, *this is Jordan, btw*

i assumed, Xander sends back, grinning despite himself. *And this way you know I'm okay with you using it*

The little dots dance up and down for a moment, then, *fair. did the nap help?*

i feel actually human now. Xander settles back

against the couch, setting his empty plate aside. *Jus tfinished dinner and i'm reading the second book before I go to bed at a reasonable hour*

suuure, Jordan replies. *I just want it on record that it's not my fault if you look like death tomorrow at the children's hospital*

Xander laughs. *noted*

There's a longer pause this time. Then finally, *well I'll let you get back to it. do I need to text you at eleven to remind you to sleep?*

probably not a bad idea, Xander sends, pretending that the idea doesn't feel intimate in a way he's not used to. He wouldn't think twice of asking Justin or Brooke to do something like that, so he's not sure why it feels different if Jordan does it. It just does.

Fine, Jordan replies.

It takes Xander awhile to get back into the book.

"GOOD JOB not looking like death today," Jordan says when Xander manages to track him down the next morning.

"Thanks," Xander grumbles, shoving Jordan's

coffee into his hands. "It was just getting to the fun part, too."

Jordan just grins at him, wide and shit-eating. "Hey, I'm not about to get fired because you can't control yourself around books. Also, not that I'm complaining, but what's up with the coffee?"

Xander shrugs, doing his level best not to start blushing. The honest truth is that he's started reflexively adding Jordan's coffee order to his, not even realizing he's done it until he drives away half the time. "Consider it a tip for all the massages this season, or a down payment on the ones that are coming."

"Okay," Jordan says slowly, but he takes a sip instead of calling Xander out on it. "That's legit. I was about to make you a frequent customer card. But seriously, man, if you keep blowing through books this fast, I'm gonna run out of things to recommend."

"Then we can move on to TV," Xander says with another shrug. "There's a lot of shows I didn't have time to watch when I was in Juniors."

Jordan nods. "Okay, that's doable. But I refuse to be held responsible for any all-night binges."

"Chirp, chirp, chirp," Xander mutters. He forgets what else he was going to say when the clock over Jordan's shoulder catches his eye. "Shit, I'd better go get my gear on. See you later?"

"You know where to find me," Jordan confirms. "Gotta earn those tips."

Xander bites back the crude response that springs instinctively to his lips, turning away with a nod. "Worth every penny," he throws back over his shoulder, Jordan's grin the last thing he sees before he heads down the hall.

"Look, I'm just saying." Jordan pauses to take a bite of his sandwich, chewing and swallowing so fast Xander is actually a little afraid he might choke. "DS9 was arguably the best Star Trek series, and I'm not just saying that because of Captain Sisko."

Xander holds up his hands. "I wouldn't dream of suggesting it."

"Good," Jordan says. "But it's unique in all of Star Trek canon. Every other series, even the new shiny disco ball, is centered around a ship, a crew that's on the move. DS9 is the only one that keeps them in one location, lets them have longer arcs that aren't just about characters' personal crises."

"But the characters are what make the show,"

Xander argues. "Even DS9 was incredibly episodic; it's just the nature of a Star Trek series. Having the characters traveling allows them to deal with a wider range of situations, which gives them more range to grow and develop. Plus, you've got to admit that the Ferengi are some pretty anti-semitic shit."

Jordan sighs. "They definitely started out that way," he concedes. "But that was something that the writers really worked hard to get away from as the series progressed. And while I'm not *just* a DS9 fan because of Sisko, having a black man as captain was huge. It's the nineties equivalent of Captain Holt on Brooklyn Nine-Nine.

"On what now?" Xander asks, confused by the sudden conversational shift.

"Oh my God," Jordan says, staring at him with something akin to horror. "You—have you not even *heard* of Brooklyn Nine-Nine?"

Xander searches his memory. "It sounds kind of familiar," he finally admits. "But I don't really know anything about it."

"That's it," Jordan says, his voice brooking no opposition. "You have homework. I'm going to expect a written one-page report on my desk by the end of the week."

"You're joking," Xander says flatly.

Jordan grins at him. "Only about the report. Trust me. You'll thank me later."

Xander opens his mouth to retort, but he's cut off by Jordan's phone buzzing on the table next to him. "Shit," he swears, looking at the screen.

"Everything okay?"

"Just forgot about a meeting," Jordan mumbles, shoving the last of his sandwich in his mouth. "Gotta run, but we're not finished with this discussion!"

He's gone before Xander can reply.

8

JORDAN

"Hey," Marian says as she sits down across from Jordan. "Where's your boyfriend?"

"Doctor's appointment for his shoulder," Jordan says absently, more than half his attention on the book he's reading. It takes a minute for Marian's words and his response to seep into his consciousness. "Wait--he's not--I'm not--"

Marian waits patiently through his sputtering, cutting neat bites off of whatever casserole her wife had sent for her lunch. "You're not what?" she asks when he finally runs down into silence without finishing a sentence.

"He's not my boyfriend," Jordan mutters, feeling fourteen again instead of twenty-six.

She raises skeptical eyebrows in his direction. "You eat lunch together every day. He brings you coffee. And you're always texting him."

"We're friends!" Jordan protests. "You know he and Justin were tight, and everybody else has their little groups already."

"If you say so." She returns her attention to her lunch. "I'm just saying, if it walks like a duck and quacks like a duck--"

Jordan rolls his eyes. "I am not--" he takes a deep breath, looks around at the players and staff eyeing them curiously, and lowers the volume of his voice to a bare whisper. "I am not dating Xander Richards. I'm not that stupid. We like the same kind of books and TV shows, and it's nice to have somebody here to talk about them. That's it."

"Okay, then."

He eyes her, not at all fooled by the bland expression on her face. But after two years of working together, despite what Marian might think, he knows a losing battle when he sees one.

"Okay," he repeats, hating the sullen note in his voice, and returns to his sandwich.

They eat in silence for a few minutes, Jordan returning to his book and Marian scrolling through something on her phone before anyone speaks again. "Do you think we need to change up Elvis' training program?" Marian asks finally, closing the empty plastic container and tucking it into her insulated lunch bag.

Jordan marks his place and purses his lips in thought. "Maybe. His cardio endurance could use some more work, but--"

His train of thought is interrupted by the buzz of the phone in his pocket. He pulls it out, glancing absently at the screen, becoming instantly distracted when he sees Xander's name.

doc says shoulder's healed, just need to keep an eye on it. i'm cleared for full workouts. glad i know a good massage therapist :)

While he's reading, another message pops up on the screen.

did you finish the cloud roads yet?

Jordan moves automatically to reply, pausing mid-text when he remembers that Marian is still sitting across from him. Sure enough, she's smirking at him, clearly projecting an air of "I told you so" without having to say a word.

"I don't want to hear it," he says flatly, looking back down at his phone

"My lips are sealed." In his peripheral vision, she mimes locking her mouth and throwing away the key.

He chooses not to respond in favor of texting Xander back. No good can possibly come of continuing this debate.

not yet. m and i are talking training plans.

cool, is the near-instant response. *tell her i wanna get my bench back up to 300*

Jordan shakes his head. *smh. do you WANT to tear something again*

he gets three eyeroll emojis back. *slowly. not stupid. but doc says i can try to get back. that's what you & m are for, right? help us be all we can be and not break ourselves*

hopefully, Jordan sends back. He hesitates over the on-screen keyboard, part of him wanting to tell Xander what Marian had said. But he still remembers the initial awkwardness, before things smoothed out. There's no point in bringing up something that will just make things awkward all over again.

i'll tell her, he finally texts. *you'll be regretting it in a week, tops*

looking forward to it! Xander replies. *oh, i down-*

loaded leverage s1 and we're watching it on the roadie.
bring your headphones for the plane

Jordan sends a thumbs-up emoji, then swears when he notices the time on his phone screen. *gtg, lunch is over*

ttyl, Xander sends back

When Jordan stuffs his phone back in his pocket and looks up, Marian is still smirking at him, but she looks a little worried around the eyes, like she's about to start lecturing him.

"Not a word," he warns, cramming the last few bites of his sandwich into his mouth and standing. She doesn't need to tell him he's being stupid.

He already knows.

JORDAN HATES himself a little for the way that his eyes go straight to Xander when he enters the weight room, but he's pretty well practiced in shoving that feeling aside by this point. Surely one of these days he'll get over it. But clearly today is not this day.

Of course, it doesn't help that Xander, as usual, has shucked his shirt off and is running around in just a pair of loose, silky shorts over his compression shorts, socks and running shoes. Despite the slightly cool temperature of the weight room, he's clearly been on the treadmill long enough to work up a sweat, a thin sheen of it covering all that exposed skin and glistening in the light.

Be a goddamn professional, Jordan tells himself fiercely as he crosses the room.

Of course, the smile that crosses Xander's face when he sees Jordan doesn't help at all. About the time Jordan gets halfway across the room, Xander's treadmill starts to slow down, his pace dropping from a run to a jog and then to a fast walk.

"Hey," Xander says when Jordan gets within earshot, pulling out one earbud, his voice slightly breathless. "Ready to help me get those gains?"

Jordan rolls his eyes, hoping that hides the affection he's feeling. "Sure. As soon as you stop saying that like you're mentally spelling it with a z."

Xander just grins wider. "No can do, sorry. But seriously, I want to work on my bench today."

"I know," Jordan says, trying to sound exasperated and pretty sure he's failing. "You texted me about it seventy times since your doctor's appointment."

"Not that many," Xander protests. "Ten at the outside."

Jordan raises an eyebrow at him. "Don't make me pull out the receipts, Richards. But yes, if you checked your email, you would've already seen the new training program Marian and I put together for you."

"You're the best," Xander says, slowing to a stop and grabbing the towel hung over the handrail to wipe the sweat off his forehead.

It's a struggle, but Jordan manages to only allow himself one quick glance at Xander's sweat-covered everything before tearing his eyes away.

"Okay," Xander says once he reemerges, grabbing his water bottle from the cup holder. "Lead the way, Coach."

"Not a coach," Jordan reminds him, turning on his heel and heading for an empty bench rack.

He can practically hear the shrug in Xander's voice. "Close enough."

"Does that mean you're going to do what I say without complaining?" Jordan asks, even though he already knows the answer.

"Not a chance," Xander replies, grabbing two forty-five pound plates off the rack and carrying them over to the bar.

Jordan shakes his head and grabs a pair of dumbbells instead. "Getting a little ahead of ourselves there, aren't we?"

Xander looks at him blankly.

Jordan sighs. "You've really got to start checking your email more often. We're starting with dumbbells first. Keeping them steady is going to use different stabilizer muscles than the bar."

"You're the boss," Xander says, returning the plates to the rack.

Much to Jordan's surprise, Xander is actually a pretty model athlete, obeying instructions without much complaint. He does chafe a little at the weight restrictions at first, but after a few sets that fades away, his forehead furrowing as he concentrates on his form and getting in the required number of reps.

If Jordan wasn't required to watch the movement of Xander's muscles for professional reasons, the whole situation would be a lot easier, but he manages to keep from drooling or letting Xander drop a dumbbell on his stupid, pretty face. So overall, the session seems to be a success.

"Well?" Xander says, sitting up on the bench as Jordan takes the dumbbells after the last set and sets them on the floor. "Think I'll make it?"

"How's your shoulder feel?" Jordan asks instead of answering directly.

Xander rotates the shoulder in question experimentally, wincing a little bit, but not looking like he's in actual pain. "A little tender, but not too bad. I think I'll live."

Jordan reaches out without thinking, then stops himself. "Can I?"

"Sure, man," Xander replies easily, turning to give Jordan better access. "Knock yourself out."

His skin is warm to the touch, but just Xander's normal body heat, not the elevated temperature that would indicate inflammation or something else dangerous. "I think you'll be okay," Jordan says after a minute of probing gently at the joint. "But if you want to come in after you've showered and have me work on it, I'm here till 5 today."

"Cool," Xander replies. He doesn't move away until Jordan drops his hand, which--Jordan needs to not be thinking about this, not be reading into that. "I'll probably do that. Nice to not have a game tonight; after you're done with me, I'm gonna go home, eat something, and then just lay on the couch until I'm ready for bed."

"That sounds like a great plan," Jordan replies. "I think I'll steal it."

Xander claps him on the shoulder. "Hey, what are friends for?"

He bends over to pick up his t-shirt and towel, which is just the unfairness cherry on top of the unfairness sundae of Jordan's life.

"I'm gonna—go get set up," Jordan says hastily, doing his best to sound normal and also not to stare at Xander's ass, miserably aware he's probably failing on both counts. "Come find me when you're ready."

He's halfway to the door when he hears Xander saying "Will do" behind him and he doesn't even care that he's running away. Honestly, there's only so much his little gay heart can be asked to handle, and a half-naked, sweaty Xander Richards is just too —everything.

Running away is the only sane option at this point.

JORDAN KNOCKS on Cammie and Emma's door before he opens it, even though they've told him that he doesn't have to, because it just feels weird to walk right in. He's pretty sure Nana would spontaneously develop teleportation abilities just to come beat his ass if she found out—and she always found out—that he was walking into people's houses without so much as a knock.

"Hello?" he calls, stepping into the empty living room and closing the door behind him. The sound of music and quiet conversation drifts in from the kitchen, along with a smell that has his stomach growling.

"In here," Cammie calls back, poking her head around the wall separating the kitchen and dining room. "Hey, stranger, long time no see."

Jordan hangs up his jacket and toes off his shoes before following his nose into the kitchen, setting the games he'd brought down on the dining table. "Yeah, well, you know how the start of the season goes," he says, accepting a hug from Cammie and then from Emma before she goes back to stirring the pot of chili. "Where's everybody else?"

"Late as usual," Emma says, the exasperation in her voice unable to hide the fondness. "I think Dan and Matt are on their way, but—"

His phone vibrates in his pocket and he pulls it out without thinking. *sos,* the text from Xander reads. *out of books. send help. urgent.*

Jordan doesn't even realize he's smiling at his screen until Emma and Cammie start making interested noises in the background. He gets the phone locked and back in his pocket, only barely evading Cammie's reaching fingers, but that doesn't protect him from the curiosity in their eyes.

"So," Cammie says, drawing the word out excessively. "Talking to someone special?"

"Just a friend from the team." Jordan does his level best to meet her eyes openly.

She exchanges a speaking glance with Emma, both of them communicating silently with their eyebrows. Jordan does his best not to crack, but they clearly studied the silent treatment from the same school as Nana.

He's opening his mouth to add something else, knowing even as he does so that he's going to be leaving himself open to an epic interrogation. Someone up there is looking out for him, though, because just then the door opens and Dan and Matt come clomping in.

"I'm just gonna—" He makes his escape into the living room before he has to finish that sentence, but as it happens, Dan does need a hand with the precarious stack of food containers. They get everything settled on the kitchen island and the table and Jordan is just breathing a sigh of relief when Emma says, "So Jordan was just telling us about his new boyfriend—"

The resulting clamor is loud and overwhelming and Jordan only barely escapes the urge to bang his head against the wall.

9

XANDER

Xander feels stupid, standing in the hotel hallway and staring at a closed door. That doesn't change the fact that he's doing it.

Just knock, he tells himself. *This is literally his job.*

His hand stays stubbornly by his side, apparently unconvinced.

He's about to just turn around and go back to his room, see if ice and Tylenol will knock out the stiffness enough to sleep, when the door opens and Jordan is standing there, ice bucket in hand.

"Hey," Jordan says. "Shoulder?"

"Yeah," Xander agrees. "Think I pushed a little too hard at practice, and then the plane—"

Jordan nods, stepping back and holding the door. "That'll do it. C'mon in and we'll see what we can do."

Xander steps obediently inside, following him down the little hall and into the room where his portable massage table is already set up. It's stupid to feel awkward. He knows this. They'd spent the entire flight to Chicago huddled together, Xander's iPad propped between their seats so they could watch Leverage. And God knows Jordan has massaged his shoulder so many times this season alone that he's lost count.

But still, he can't help feeling self-conscious as he strips off his t-shirt, more aware of Jordan's eyes on his skin than he usually is. Even the residual ache in his shoulder isn't enough to distract him from it. Maybe it's the change of setting, the big king-size bed so close behind him. Instead of climbing onto the table, he could just step backward, sprawl across the covers—

He forces himself to stop following that train of thought as he climbs onto the table, his half-hard cock obvious in his shorts even though neither of them mentions it.

"It might be easier if you lie down," Jordan says, his voice a little lower than usual, a little rougher—

or maybe that's just wishful thinking. "On your back to start."

Xander nods, any response he might have made getting stuck in his throat. Swinging his legs up onto the table, he lowers himself down as directed, waiting while Jordan retrieves a pump bottle of something from his bag and squirts a little into his hands.

Only supreme force of will keeps him from jumping when Jordan touches him. It's not like it's a surprise. Not like he's unfamiliar with the warmth of Jordan's hands, the slick feeling of the massage oil. It's just different somehow. More—intimate, maybe, in the hushed quiet and dim light of the hotel room, so different from the trainers room with it's open door and harsh overhead fluorescents.

"There?" Jordan asks quietly, pressing on a tender spot.

Xander hisses between his teeth. He knows that tensing up is counterproductive, but it's a fight to keep it from happening. "Yeah," he breathes, forcing himself to relax.

Jordan hums sympathetically, but he doesn't let up, working away the tension with fingers, knuckles, the heel of his hand and, for several particularly torturous moments, his elbow. It's a small eternity before he lifts his hands, leaving Xander limp, except for his still stupidly hopeful cock, and shaking on the table.

"You can turn over now," Jordan says, tactfully not commenting on the state Xander is in or the awkward way his cock bobs under his shorts as he turns over.

His face is still flaming by the time he gets it settled in the little round pillow thing. But then Jordan's hands are on him again and all he can do is try—and fail—to keep his moans from sounding sexual.

It hurts, of course it does. His muscles are knotted tight and aching with it, and Jordan is the furthest thing from gentle. Xander's never considered himself a masochist, but he's starting to wonder if maybe he should rethink that conclusion. It's taking every ounce of willpower he possesses to keep from grinding his now fully-hard cock down against the massage table until he comes in his shorts. As it is, Jordan's massage moves him around enough to keep a continual, torturous friction going.

By the time Jordan's finished, Xander is giving serious consideration to whimpering. Or begging. Or possibly just asking for a couple of minutes alone, because that's seriously about all it will take. Maybe not even that long. Instead he closes his eyes, takes deep breaths and does his best to will his stupid, idiot cock into submission.

"You okay?" Jordan asks, his voice so soft it's barely audible.

"Yeah," Xander says, pushing up to sit with his back to Jordan. Like that's all it'll take to keep from embarrassing himself. He rolls his shoulder by way of distracting both of them, slumping with relief when the muscles move freely. "That's really good. Thanks."

"No problem."

Xander waits a few more seconds, but his cock seems quite happy to stay like it is, so he gives up and pushes to his feet, doing his best to keep his lower body angled away from Jordan as he heads toward the door. "I'll see you tomorrow?"

"Wait—"

He's turning before he even realizes he started moving, only noticing his mistake when Jordan sucks in a sharp breath. He can feel the heat spreading across his face again, down his neck. But all that seems immaterial when he sees Jordan, standing there, holding out Xander's forgotten shirt —with a very distinct bulge in his own pants.

"Thanks," Xander mutters, taking one step, then another, until he's close enough to reach for his shirt, his eyes locked on Jordan's. Close enough to think longingly of dropping it to the floor, of pushing Jordan down onto the bed and just taking what they both want.

His fingers loosen on the fabric, but then he remembers Jordan saying, "I don't just want a fuck." The heat under his skin goes nuclear as he realizes he was about to throw himself at someone who already shot him down.

Xander turns on his heel, his fist clenching around the shirt. "Thanks," he says again, his voice a strange, choked thing that he doesn't recognize. "I'll see you in the morning."

Any reply Jordan might have made is lost when the door clicks shut behind him. He pulls the shirt over his head with hands that are definitely not shaking and makes his way back to his own room.

IT'S LATE ENOUGH that he should be sleeping or at least getting ready to, but Xander can't settle. Jordan's voice in his head is an endless, inescapable loop. He tries reading but gives up after realizing he's reread the same page four times without absorbing any of it. TV is also a bust, 300 channels and nothing to watch.

He pulls out his phone, wincing at the time. But Seattle is playing Vancouver tomorrow, so Justin's probably up. Just to be on the safe side, he shoots off a text—*hey u up?*—instead of immediately opening Skype; the last thing he needs is Brooke mad at him for interrupting her husband time.

In this one thing at least, tonight is his lucky night, because Justin texts back immediately. *ya, skype?*

Instead of answering with a text, Xander flips to the Skype app and starts the call. It connects a few seconds later, Justin grinning back at him from the screen.

"What's up?" he asks curiously, settling back against the pillows in his nearly-identical hotel room. "Figured you'd be in bed by now."

"I am in bed," Xander points out, because if you can't be a pedantic asshole with your best friend, who can you be one with? "Can't sleep. Figured your ugly face might shock me into it."

Justin rolls his eyes, but that doesn't disguise the

fondness in them. "Yeah, yeah. What's keeping you awake? Girl troubles? Boy troubles?"

Xander shifts uncomfortably against the sheets. He's suddenly reminded of exactly how disconcerting it is when Justin quits acting like a lovable goofball and actually uses his brain. "Who says it's either?"

"Well, your face, for starters," Justin replies blandly. "C'mon, tell Uncle Justin what's wrong."

Xander shudders. "If you promise never to call yourself that again, maybe I'll talk to you."

"Awww." Justin mock-pouts into the camera. "But what are your kids supposed to call me?"

"You're such an asshole," Xander says, laughing helplessly. "Why are we friends again?"

The pout transforms into a satisfied grin. "Because I actually put up with your whiny ass. Now seriously. Talk, or I'm hanging up and watching porn before I go to bed."

"Nothing big," Xander says, picking at the duvet with his thumb and forefinger. "Really, literally nothing. Nothing happened."

"But you wanted something to happen?" Justin holds up his free hand defensively when Xander glares at him. "I'm just guessing, man. You don't have to talk to me if you don't want to. But if it's keeping you up, maybe it'd be better to get it out."

Xander thumps his head lightly back against the pillows, then again harder. It's not very satisfying. "I feel like I'm taking crazy pills," he mutters.

"Okay, stop me when I'm wrong," Justin says after a few minutes of silence. "So you've been hanging out with *Darling*—"

The way he drags out the name has Xander glaring into the phone camera again.

Justin ignores him, of course, because he's the literal worst. "So you two have been doing friend stuff. But you still think he's hot and you want to fuck him. Except he said no. How'm I doing so far?"

"I hate you," Xander groans. At this rate his cheeks are just going to be permanently the color of a tomato.

"No you don't," Justin says easily. "You hate that I'm right."

"I can do both." Xander scrubs his free hand over his face. "Fuck. Seriously, fuck me. I can't even get a massage without getting a half-chub going. Or more."

Justin starts laughing. He does try to stop when Xander gives him a look, but it doesn't do much good. "Dude. No, I'm sorry, I'm sorry, I know that's terrible, but you have to admit it's fucking funny."

"It's funny when it's not happening to you," Xander retorts. "You weren't laughing back when you were pining over Brooke."

"Hey, that's different."

It's Xander's turn to smirk at the camera. "Oh yeah? How is it different?"

"It just is," Justin huffs. "I'm married, so clearly I have more game than you."

"What the fuck ever. Go to sleep, you're clearly delirious with exhaustion."

Justin rolls his eyes. "Maybe I will. You quit pining and go to sleep too. You'll need your rest if we're gonna play against each other in the finals."

"I'm not listening," Xander sing-songs, flipping Justin off as he ends the call.

It really is late, and he's feeling a lot more settled in his skin, even if Justin is the least helpful friend of all time. Xander sets his phone on the bedside table and turns off the light, settling back against the pillows.

Darkness fills the hotel room, broken only by the light seeping through around the edges of the drawn curtains. He does his best to empty his mind, to let himself drift off, but his mind is full of Jordan. The sense-memory of Jordan's hands on his skin is so vivid it feels like a hallucination, and Xander groans as his cock begins to fill again.

This problem, at least, is simple enough to deal with. He shoves the covers aside to keep from getting them messy, then licks his palm and wraps his hand around his cock, the foreskin sliding slickly over the sensitive head. He tries to think about Nick, getting bent over the bed and fucked while he begs for it. He tries to think about that one couple, whatever their names were, about being fucked between them. He tries to think about celebrities, hot, anonymous strangers.

But his mind, his stupid, traitorous mind, keeps coming back to the dim, intimate space of Jordan's hotel room. Keeps whispering "what if?" What if he'd stripped off all his clothes instead of just his shirt? What if he'd stretched out on the massive king-sized bed instead of climbing up on the massage table?

He licks his lips, keeping the movement of his hand over his cock slow and even. This isn't for him, not entirely. He's putting on a show, and judging from the look in Jordan's eyes, the bulge in his pants, he doesn't mind a bit.

"You just going to watch?" he asks, his voice low and rough. "Or do you want to join me?"

"I don't know," Jordan drawls, leaning back against the massage table. "I do like watching you. Do you take requests?"

Xander's whole body flashes hot at the question. "You want to tell me what to do?"

"Do you want me to?" Jordan counters, like his cock didn't twitch in his pants at the question.

"Try it and see." Xander smirks up at him, letting his body roll a little bit, letting himself fuck up into the circle of his fist.

Jordan hums low in the back of his throat, considering. "Touch yourself."

Xander raises his eyebrows. "Thought I was?"

"Not just your cock," Jordan says, his voice patient. "Are your nipples sensitive?"

Almost reflexively, Xander's free hand strokes up his stomach, over his chest, his eyes fluttering closed as his thumb brushes over his nipple. He forces them back open, not wanting to miss a minute of watching Jordan. "Yeah," he breathes, trailing his fingers across to the other one.

"Good," Jordan rasps. "Again."

Xander would be more embarrassed about how he writhes against the bedsheets if it didn't feel so fucking good. *"Want to see you, too,"* he pants, *his whole body shaking with the need to come.*

"You first," Jordan says, *pressing the heel of his hand against his cock. "Wanna watch you come all over yourself, get yourself filthy—"*

Xander bites his lip as he comes, trying desperately to keep quiet as he shakes through his orgasm. It's so good, the crest of pleasure, the moment of clarity in the aftermath, that he almost doesn't feel guilty for jerking off to a fantasy of his friend.

Almost.

He wipes off with tissues from the bedside table and pulls the blanket back over himself. His body is tired now, worn out from a long day and pleasantly relaxed from the endorphins flooding his brain. Maybe *now* he can fall asleep.

It's only as he's drifting off to sleep when he realizes that, for the first time in years, he'd had a conversation with Justin without that desperate, lost ache in his chest. He pulls up the memory of the Skype call, replaying it. Nothing had really changed; there was nothing different about the way they talked or gave each other shit. The only difference is Xander's feelings.

Shit, if Xander can get over his unattainable best friend, maybe anything is possible.

JORDAN

"Hey," Xander says, sliding into the chair across from Jordan and opening his lunch.

"You doing okay?" Jordan asks. "That was a pretty rough hit during practice."

Xander shrugs, but both his shoulders are moving freely, so he's probably actually okay. "It probably looked worse than it was."

"If you say so." Jordan tries to keep the skepticism out of his voice, but he's pretty sure he fails.

They eat in silence for a few minutes. Jordan opens his mouth a couple of times to speak, then closes it, hating himself for the swirl of nerves in his gut. *You're friends,* he tells himself firmly. *This is a thing that friends do. Ask him!*

"So," he finally says, forcing the word out through a throat gone tight. "The series premier of *Dragonfly* is on Tuesday."

"That's right!" Xander looks up from his food. "Shit, is that next week?"

Jordan nods. "I was wondering if you wanted to come over and watch it?"

"Sure," Xander says easily, like he has no idea of the turmoil going on in Jordan's head. "I can bring food if you want?"

"I've got it, but if you want to help cook, I could always use an extra set of hands?"

Xander grins. "Deal. And I'll bring the beer."

"Great." Jordan closes his teeth before anything about it being a date escapes him. This is not a date. This is friends. They're friends.

"Great," Xander echoes, his eyes crinkling as he smiles.

Jordan can't help but smile back, despite the sinking sensation in the pit of his stomach.

He is so fucked.

"Okay," Jordan says, setting the cooked chicken on the plates with the roasted asparagus and potatoes.

"We've got five minutes. I'll grab these. You wanna get the beer out of the fridge?"

Xander tosses him an odd little salute before heading to the fridge. "Can do."

Jordan picks up the plates and heads for the couch, doing his best not to stare. He's seen Xander bloody and bruised after a fight, sweaty and stripped down, dressed in his suit for press. But something about this, about Xander in his space, casual in a faded green henley that turns his skin and hair to shades of gold—it's soft and intimate, settling inside Jordan's chest with an ache he can't ignore.

"All right," Xander says briskly, settling down on the other end of the couch and popping the tops off the beers before handing one to Jordan. "Let's do this."

Jordan turns on the TV and flips it to the appropriate channel, hopelessly aware that his chances of focusing on the show are almost nonexistent. He takes a long drink of his beer, staring blankly at the commercials flashing on the screen one after the other.

Next to him, Xander drinks from his own beer, head tipped back, mouth obscene where it fits to the neck of the bottle. The appreciative noise falling from his lips as he sets the beer down is even worse, sending heat flashing through Jordan's body.

Setting his beer down on the side table, Jordan reaches blindly for his plate, nearly jumping out of his seat when his hand brushes against Xander's.

"Shit," Xander laughs, taking his plate and settling back against the couch cushions. "Sorry, I— uh, I wasn't looking."

"Me either," Jordan manages, his throat suddenly tight. This is fucking ridiculous. He wasn't even this awkward in high school, for fuck's sake.

Thankfully, the show starts just then, success-fully distracting both of them with a world far away from their own. Despite the lingering tension in he room, Jordan finds himself getting drawn into the story, invested in the teenage protagonists and the desperate quest to save their world.

By the time the premiere is over, with at least four commercial breaks full of debating different speculation with Xander, he's almost forgotten his earlier discomfort. At least, until Xander gets to his feet, wincing and rolling his shoulder tentatively. His limited range of motion would make the stiff-ness obvious even if Jordan hadn't learned to read his body language since the start of the season.

"Want me to take a look at that before you head

home?" The words are out before he can stop them, hanging there in the air, impossible to take back.

Xander licks his lips, his eyes wide. "Uh, yeah? That—you don't have to."

Jordan shrugs, doing his best to look casual. "No point in you suffering all night when I can do something about it."

"Yeah, okay." Xander looks back at the couch. "Here?"

"Uh, no." Jordan winces at the thought of what it would do to his back to try and work on something so low. "I—this way."

As he turns to walk toward his bedroom, Xander's footfalls following behind him, he can't ignore the little voice in his head telling him that this is stupid. A bad idea.

He just doesn't care.

It's just a massage, Jordan tells himself desperately, as Xander strips off his shirt and sits on the side of the bed, uncharacteristically silent. Just the same thing they've been doing since training camp. On his *bed*, fuck his entire *life*.

"Just a sec," he says quietly, disappearing into

his bathroom to grab the lightly scented lotion he keeps on the counter, avoiding eye contact with his reflection. When he comes back out into the bedroom, Xander is still waiting, his eyes dark and intent as they watch him cross to the bed.

"Anything different?" Jordan asks, mostly to fill the silence. It's unnerving, having all of Xander's attention focused on him. Having Xander here, in his private space. "Anything that's hurting more than usual?"

Xander shakes his head, his voice just as soft when he answers. "No. Just, you know."

Jordan nods, reaching out. He's vaguely surprised that his hands don't shake, but they move over Xander's shoulder with the ease of familiarity. As familiar as the noises Xander makes, breathy and suggestive and somehow overwhelming in the quiet of the room.

After a few minutes of stretching awkwardly, Jordan finally acknowledges defeat and climbs up to kneel on the mattress. It's the only practical choice, he knows this. The fact that it puts him in close proximity to Xander, that it makes the situation almost unbearably intimate—well, that's just a fucking bonus, isn't it?

By the time he's worked loose all the knotted

muscles in the front of Xander's shoulder, Jordan is doing his best to ignore the ache where his cock presses against his zipper, hard and insistent. "Let me get a towel before you lie down," he says, sliding down to the floor. "So I don't get lotion all over my bed."

He disappears into the bathroom before Xander can respond, doing his best to focus on one task at a time and not on how truly, deeply fucked he is. Right now he needs a towel. Thankfully he did laundry last weekend, so there are actually several clean towels in the cabinet for a change.

Once towels are retrieved, he only hesitates for a few seconds before returning to the bedroom. Xander was busy in his absence, it seems, pulling the duvet and top sheet down to the foot of the bed.

"I thought—" he pauses, starts again. "Sheets are easier to wash?"

"Good call," Jordan agrees briskly, spreading the towels over the mattress. "Okay, all set."

Seriously, though, fuck his entire life. He has no idea who he pissed off in a past life, but surely it wasn't bad enough to deserve this, watching Xander crawl half-naked into his bed, sprawling across the dark gray towels and sheets like something out of porn.

He takes a deep, hopefully quiet, breath before climbing onto the mattress. *Halfway done,* he tells himself, pumping more lotion, rubbing it between his palms to warm it. Not stalling. *Just a little longer and he'll go home and you can go jerk off in the shower.*

It's hard—ha!—to remember that, though. When Xander goes boneless under the first touch of Jordan's hands, when he actually, literally moans, low and needy, into the mattress—it takes every ounce of willpower Jordan possesses to keep his touch professional. But he grits his teeth and does it.

Between the slightly awkward angle—it would be so much easier just to straddle Xander's waist, but that way lies madness—and the constant distraction of his cock, it takes Jordan a few minutes to realize that Xander's little rustling movements are purposeful, not just random. But then Xander whimpers, "Please," so quiet it's barely audible, his hips grinding down against the mattress again.

Every good intention in Jordan's head evaporates in a white-hot flash, like a lightning strike searing through him. "Fuck," he mutters, his hands tightening reflexively on Xander's shoulder before he forces them to loosen, to urge Xander over onto his back.

"Sorry," Xander breathes, his eyes squeezed shut for a minute before they open. "I'm sorry, I'll-I'll go, okay, just—"

Jordan lifts a hand to cup the side of his face, stubble prickling lightly against his palm and leans in, pausing just for a moment, just to be sure.

Xander's eyes widen, but he tips his chin up, lips parted and welcoming. "Yeah?"

"Yeah." Jordan closes the last, tiny space between them, capturing Xander's lips with his just as they start to turn up a little at the corners. It's a surprisingly gentle kiss, despite the hunger roaring through his body, just the soft press of their mouths together, his hand on Xander's face their only other point of contact. He pulls back, just a little, just enough to realize that he's never seen Xander look this soft, this open.

He's not sure which of them moves first, if Xander surges up or if he leans down, but their second kiss is hot and wet and filthy, fighting to devour each other with lips and teeth and tongues. Xander pulls him down, both of them groaning into the kiss when Jordan's weight settles on top of him, and slides big, warm hands up under Jordan's shirt.

Eventually they have to break apart to breathe, sucking in big gulps of air, and Xander wastes no time dragging Jordan's shirt up further. "Off," he demands, not stopping until the fabric is bunched under his arms. "Why are you still dressed?"

Jordan sits up and pulls the shirt up over his head. He has no idea where it ends up, distracted by Xander's eyes on his bare chest, the hard line of Xander's cock grinding up against his ass. "You're —" he temporarily loses track of what he was saying when Xander starts unbuttoning his jeans. "You're still wearing pants too."

"Ugh, yeah. Somebody should fix that."

Xander's hands keep moving, though, pulling down the zipper. Jordan sucks in a breath as the pressure against his cock is relieved, then again when Xander's hand slips in and gives him one long, lingering stroke through the fabric of his boxer briefs.

"You're not giving me much incentive to get up and get your pants off," he points out, unable to keep himself from thrusting into Xander's hand, just a little bit.

"You want incentive?" Xander grins wickedly,

licking his lips. "Once we're both naked, I want to blow you."

The mental picture is enough to have Jordan whimpering, scrambling gracelessly off the bed to shove his jeans and boxer briefs down his legs. He's vaguely aware that maybe his eagerness should be embarrassing, but Xander is moving just as fast, stripping off his pants and boxers, pushing Jordan down to sit on the side of the bed. He slides to his knees between Jordan's spread legs, and this is it, this is how Jordan dies.

"Condom?" he asks, looking up at Jordan from under those stupid, unfair eyelashes.

"Oh, uh, yeah." Jordan leans over to pull open the drawer on his bedside table, trying desperately to remember if he even still has any condoms. In his defense, it's hard to think when all the blood in his body has drained into his cock, when Xander's hands are stroking absently up and down his thighs.

Fate has apparently decided to smile on him, though, because his searching fingers find a condom packet almost immediately. He goes to open it, but Xander takes it out of his hands before he can, ripping it open and rolling it down Jordan's cock in one efficient movement.

"This okay?" he asks, like there's even the ghost

of a chance that Jordan might say no. He's gorgeous and obscene like this, naked and on his knees in front of Jordan, lips parted like there's nothing he wants more than Jordan's cock in his mouth.

"Fuck, yes," Jordan breathes, reaching out to touch his face. "Unless you don't—"

The rest of the sentence is lost when Xander's mouth closes over the head of his cock, the heat and suction overwhelming even through the latex barrier. He doesn't pause, sliding down, down, his lips tight against the shaft. Jordan's hand slides around to cup the back of his head instinctively, but he lets go as soon as he realizes what he was doing, pressing both hands down hard against the mattress.

Xander pulls off at that, looking incredibly smug. Jordan would resent it if he wasn't so desperately aroused. "You can grab my hair," he says quietly, wrapping his hand around the base of Jordan's cock and jerking him with slow, torturous strokes. "I like it."

He ducks back down before Jordan can react to his words, sliding down until his lips meet the place where his hand is curled around the base of Jordan's cock.

"Fuck," Jordan chokes out, lifting a tentative hand to thread through his hair. "Really?"

He shoots Jordan an impatient look, bobbing his head so fast that it tugs on the strands of hair caught between Jordan's fingers. The moan it elicits vibrates around Jordan's cock, adding another incredible dimension to the layers of sensation driving him higher.

"Okay." Jordan barely recognizes his voice, already rough and wrecked like he's the one on his knees with a cock pushing into his throat—fuck, that mental image is not going to help his stamina *at all.* He tightens his hand gently, pulling lightly on Xander's hair. Xander rewards him with another moan, another slide down, another swirl of his tongue along the shaft. "Fuck, fuck, you're—good at that."

The look he gets this time is unmistakably smug, especially when Xander takes him in that last inch, nose bumping gently against Jordan's skin. He pauses there for an endless moment before pulling back, sucking in air through his nose while Jordan resists the urge to fuck up into his mouth. Then he does it again.

"Fuck." Jordan feels dimly that he should be embarrassed by how his vocabulary has narrowed down to that single word, by how close he is to coming. But his attention has narrowed down too, filled with nothing but Xander. Xander's lashes fluttering as he moves, moaning like there's nothing he wants more in the world that Jordan's cock in his mouth. Xander's hands, one on Jordan's thigh, the other sliding down to stroke teasing fingertips over his balls. "Fuck, I'm not gonna—I'm so fucking close—yes, fuck, like that—"

Xander's moans take on a distinctly encouraging tone as he speeds up, fucking his mouth onto Jordan's cock until he comes, his hips thrusting forward and his fist tightening despite his best intentions. He's vaguely aware that Xander rides it out, moving with him, but the rest of the world around them could have disappeared for all he knows.

When awareness of his body returns, it's to look down as Xander slides off his cock, sitting back on his heels and smirking contentedly despite the fact that he's still visibly hard, his cock flushed red and curving up toward his belly. His hair is all over the place, his lips wet and swollen. He looks fucking *debauched* and Jordan can't even be embarrassed at the surge of pride that brings him.

"C'mere, he says, slipping the condom off and tying a knot in it before tossing it in the trash can. Xander just looks at him, so Jordan reaches out, pulls until he's close enough to kiss, to touch. Until Jordan can get his hands all over that body in a very unprofessional capacity.

"What do you want?" he breathes between kisses, catching Xander's earlobe between his teeth, sliding his hands down to wrap around Xander's waist, to get two handfuls of hockey ass.

Xander sucks in a breath, his hips grinding forward. "Anything," he rasps, shuddering under Jordan's touch. "Your hand—touch me. I'm so fucking close—"

He cuts off with a whimper when Jordan gets a hand between them and wraps it around his cock. The foreskin isn't exactly a surprise; Jordan was looking, earlier, but he hadn't thought about the difference in jerking off. Still, it means he doesn't have to pause to dig out the lube. He starts slow, learning Xander's cues: the way he bites his lip and his head falls back, his fingertips digging into Jordan's arms, the shudders rippling through his whole body.

"Tell me what you need," Jordan begs. Watching Xander is hot enough that his cock is making a valiant effort to get hard again, but he wants this to be good for Xander, too. If this is all he gets—he shoves the thought away. "Tell me what you want."

"Tighter," Xander breathes, his voice barely audible. He fucks up into Jordan's hand, shudders rippling through his body. "Fuck, please —so close—"

Jordan tightens his grip and strokes faster, getting his free hand into Xander's hair and tugging gently. "Come on, you gonna come for me—"

Xander comes with a groan, shooting slick and messy all over Jordan's chest, coating his fist as he thrusts up into it. He slumps forward when he goes still, his forehead on Jordan's shoulder, his heart pounding against Jordan's skin

For several long minutes they sit like that, their breathing slowing to normal. Long enough that reality sets back in. Long enough that Jordan really starts to realize exactly how stupid he's been. Not only does he have to see Xander every day for his job, not only was he stupid enough to make friends with him, but now he went and had sex with him? It's like a "How to not get over your crush," guide. Step by fucking step.

His self-recriminating spiral gets interrupted when Xander finally lifts his head, making a face at the mess of semen and sweat smeared between their chests. "Ugh."

"You said it," Jordan agrees, desperate to get them back to some kind of normalcy. "Shower?"

"You can go first," Xander offers, looking almost shy, as if that wasn't completely incongruous with his personality. "Since it's kinda my fault."

Jordan nudges Xander gently to his feet before standing, keeping him close with a hand on his waist. "Nah, there's room for both of us. The shower's the whole reason I picked this place. C'mon."

Xander follows him into the bathroom without talking, giving Jordan plenty of time to wonder if he's breaking some unspoken rule of one-night stands. *Fuck it,* he decides, stepping into the massive tiled stall with it's dual showerheads and waiting until Xander finishes washing his hands before turning on the water. *I already fucked him. If I only get one night, might as well make the most of it.*

"You weren't kidding," Xander says, joining him under the spray. "This thing is bigger than my closet, never mind my shower."

Jordan shrugs, turning so that the water sluices over his chest. The sticky mess on his skin is already partially dried; he has to grab a washcloth and some body wash and scrub at it. "Old habit. I'm not playing any more, but I still work out when I get a chance and it's nice to just stand under the spray, you know."

"Oh, I know," Xander agrees.

Looking back over his shoulder, Jordan realizes his mistake almost as soon as he makes it, but he's mesmerized, unable to look away. It's not just Xander's naked body, although that's nice, the way the water accentuates every muscle in his torso and arms, bunching and releasing as he scrubs himself clean. If Jordan were a couple of years younger, he's pretty sure he'd be up for round two already.

But it's the domesticity of the scene that has his chest aching. It would be so easy to pretend, if he was interested in lying to himself. To pretend that Xander is going to stay, that this is just the first of many times. That they're going to try off and go curl around each other in Jordan's bed. That this is something he can have.

He's going to leave, Jordan tells himself savagely, turning his face into the spray. *He got what he wanted from you. He'll be nice about it, but he's going to leave. And you don't get to whine about it, because you knew this was coming and you had sex with him anyway.*

"Think I'm gonna get out. You good?" he asks without turning around.

"Yeah," Xander agrees, following him out of the shower and accepting the towel Jordan hands him.

It's a strange sort of calm, Jordan thinks, drying himself mechanically and pulling on a clean pair of boxer briefs. But it just has to last until Xander leaves. After that it won't matter how emotional he is, because no one will be there to see.

He waits for Xander to get dressed, to extricate himself. He waits while Xander puts his boxers back on and settles on the bed, looking at Jordan expectantly until he stretches out next to him. He waits while Xander wraps around him, saying "I like to cuddle," in a voice that falls half-way between defiant and apologetic.

He's still waiting when the lights are out and Xander asks, his voice smaller than Jordan has ever heard it, "This okay?"

Jordan's waiting, but he can't bring himself to lie.

"Yeah."

"Cool."

Even when he slips into sleep, warm and wrapped up in Xander, a part of him is still waiting.

11

XANDER

Xander wakes up slowly, as usual, confused for a moment when he first opens his eyes. Nothing is where it should be in his room, because this isn't his room. This is Jordan's room, Jordan's bed, Jordan's clock agreeing with the thin, early morning light that there's still time to go back to sleep. Jordan's arm, heavy and comforting where it's draped over Xander's waist. Jordan's breath, warm on the back of his neck. Jordan's cock, hard and hot and pressed up against his ass, the small of his back.

He can't resist pushing back a little further, smiling a little at the noise that rumbles out of Jordan's throat. "You awake?" he whispers, rolling his hips back again.

Jordan makes some kind of unintelligible noise, his arm tightening around Xander's waist, but not otherwise reacting.

It's probably rude to wake him up, so Xander doesn't. But Jordan isn't the only one who's hard, and Xander is perfectly capable of taking care of things himself.

He slides his hand over his chest and slowly down, teasing a little, since he has time. Bypassing his cock the first time, he drags slow fingertips up his thigh, shivering as goosebumps rise on his skin. When he finally gives in, wrapping a hand around his cock, his indrawn breath sounds loud in his ears.

"Starting without me?" Jordan mumbles, pressing closer and sliding a sleepy hand down Xander's arm.

"Didn't want to wake you," Xander murmurs back.

Jordan's lips are curved when they press against the back of his neck. "Well, I'm awake now. Gonna make it worth my while?"

Xander shivers when Jordan rocks his hips, cock sliding against his ass. "You can fuck me. If you want," he blurts out without thinking.

He doesn't get a chance to regret his words

before Jordan's grip on his wrist tenses. "You—you have practice today."

"As long as you don't skip the lube, I'll be fine," Xander says, managing not to roll his eyes somehow. "Trust me."

For one long moment, he's half-convinced Jordan's going to shoot him down. Then—

"Fuck." Jordan's voice is low and rough, fervent in his ear. "Stuff's in the drawer by you."

Xander rolls until he can reach the drawer handle, Jordan's grip lingering on his wrist before letting go. It only takes a minute to dig out the mostly-full lube bottle and a condom packet. He hesitates for a minute when he sees the toys in the back of the drawer, but as intriguing as they look, that's not what he wants right now.

"Get lost?" Jordan asks, his tone wry and amused.

"Nah." Xander closes the drawer and rolls back over. Jordan looks incredible in the soft morning light, sprawled across his sheets one hand stroking idly over his cock, meeting Xander's eyes unashamedly. "How are we doing this?"

Jordan shrugs. "You started this. How do you want to do it?"

That overly casual attitude is just not going to

do it. Xander plasters himself to Jordan's side, runs a teasing hand up his thigh and over his hip. Drops a kiss on the corner of his mouth and leans in to murmur in his ear. "Want you to open me up—you have any idea how long I've been waiting to get those hands inside me? Fuck me open with your fingers first, then your cock."

"Jesus fuck." Jordan slides a hand around the back of his neck and pulls him in for a hard, hungry kiss.

"Is that a yes?" Xander teases breathlessly when they break apart, going easily when Jordan pushes him back down to the sheets, taking the lube from his hand.

Jordan just nods, applying lube to his fingers with the same intent focus he usually brings to his job. "Like you even have to ask."

Whatever retort Xander might have made is lost along with his breath when Jordan leans down and kisses his hipbone, cheek brushing with agonizing lightness against his hard, aching cock. He spreads his legs instinctively when Jordan's hand ghosts up the inside of his thigh, shivering at the first teasing touch of a slick fingertip against his hole, then again when Jordan settles between them, nudging them wider still.

The tease continues for what feels like forever, Jordan's finger pressing and retreating but never quite slipping inside until Xander rolls his hips up, chasing more sensation and moaning when he gets it. It's muffled by the arm he throws over his face, because if he watches Jordan fingering him he'll come before they even get to the good part.

Even so, it's loud enough that Jordan hears it, reaching up to push his arm off his face. "Let me hear you," he orders, only softening it after a moment with a "please."

"You might—oh fuck—regret that," Xander pants, trying to breathe. Jordan has one big finger worked inside him as deep as it can go. It's good, it's so good, but it's not quite enough. Not what he needs. Or, well, not all of what he needs. "I've been told I can—oh, God, right fucking there—get a little mouthy."

"I like your mouth," Jordan says simply. "I like knowing you like this. You want this. Come on. Talk to me."

Xander throws his head back on the pillow, his eyes fluttering shut. "Fuck. Give me another finger. I'm ready."

Jordan hums, considering. "So demanding. Is that how you ask for things?"

"Fuck." Xander swallows, hard. If he doesn't acknowledge the shiver that rocked through his body at those words, it didn't happen, right? "Please, give me another finger. I can take it."

Another thoughtful hum. He's about to give in, to beg, when he hears the bottle cap click open, feels Jordan pull his finger out, then push back in with two. It's a stretch; Jordan's fingers are thicker than his, can go deeper. It's so fucking good Xander could almost cry.

"How's that?" Jordan asks, his voice lower, rougher than before. "Come on. Talk to me, Xander."

"Good." Xander rocks his hips up to meet Jordan's hand, moans a little when Jordan's fingertips just barely graze his prostate. "So fucking good, Jordy. Think I'm ready? Or do—fuck—do I need one more? Get me—shit—get me ready for that big cock?"

Jordan swears, scissoring his fingers apart until all Xander can do is breathe through the stretch. "God, your fucking mouth—"

"Yeah," Xander interrupts, arching his body up off the bed. When he risks a peek, Jordan looks wrecked already, biting his lower lip, his face and chest sheened with sweat. "Felt so good in my mouth last night, so big and hard. Can't fucking wait to get it inside me again."

When Jordan pulls his fingers out, it leaves him feeling so empty he can't help but whine at the loss. Jordan rips the condom packet open, rolling it on in one sure motion, and shifts forward, lining himself up—only to pause.

"Is this—do you want to be on top?" he asks, his eyes not quite meeting Xander's.

Xander curls a leg around his waist by way of answer, pulling him closer. "Maybe next time. Right now I want you to fuck me into the mattress."

Jordan shudders all over, pushing inside in one slow, measured movement.

Xander has to close his eyes and breathe again, relaxing into the incredible, perfect stretch. "Fuck—yeah—" he groans, reaching up to curl his hands around Jordan's biceps. "God—feels so fucking good—"

Despite his request, Jordan sets a slow, measured pace to begin with, each deliberate stroke lighting up his nerves from the inside out. "Yeah?"

"Yeah—" Xander rocks his hips up, trying to get more, deeper. "So good, Jordy—fuck, right fucking there—"

"God," Jordan breathes, leaning down to brace

his hands on the mattress, both of them moaning from the changed angle. "Fuck—"

The change in position has Xander's cock trapped between their bodies, the friction adding another layer of incredible sensation. He digs his fingertips into Jordan's arms, throws his head back on the pillow, little helpless noises falling from his mouth with each hard, deep thrust.

"Yeah." Jordan's breath is coming harder now. "Let me—fuck—let me hear you—"

"Oh, fuck—" Xander chokes out. "I'm—fuck—so close—don't stop—"

Jordan shakes his head a little. "Not gonna—come on, come for me—"

"Fuck—" is all Xander can get out before he comes, shaking apart as Jordan fucks him relentlessly through it. By the time Jordan's steady rhythm falters, his thrusts going erratic as he pushes deep and comes, Xander feels boneless, like he could melt into the mattress and not even care.

Jordan is still braced above him, head hanging low, chest heaving like he's just been bag-skated. Xander lifts his arms, vaguely surprised that they still seem to work, and pulls at him until Jordan gives in.

"I'm heavy," he protests, making a face when the cooling mess squishes between them.

"Shut up, I don't care," Xander mutters, closing his eyes. "Still early, don't have to get up yet."

Jordan huffs out a half-laugh, but sets his head down on Xander's shoulder and doesn't protest again.

He really is heavy, but it's nice. Calm, getting pressed into the mattress like this. Xander thinks absently that it'll suck when he has to move.

It does, but after a minute Jordan comes back and wraps an arm around him, pulling him close. The next thing he knows, an alarm is going off, loud and jarring in his ear.

"C'mon, Richards," Jordan grumbles, nudging him toward the edge of the bed. "If you're late for practice, you'll get me fired."

"So what I'm hearing is that we should shower together," Xander says, enjoying the way Jordan's eyes linger on him as he stretches.

Jordan shakes his head, but he's smiling as he follows Xander into the bathroom.

ELVIS LETS out an exaggerated wolf-whistle when Xander strips out of his t-shirt to get dressed for practice. "Jesus, Richie. Pick up a vampire last night?"

Xander just shrugs, pulling his compression gear out of his bag. "You know how it is."

"We know how it is for you," Sasha agrees, smirking. "What this time? Girl? Guy? One of each?"

Xander rolls his eyes. "None of your fucking business, Ivanov. Get your rocks off some other way."

"No morning sex?" Harty asks, mock-sympathetic. "Or was it just that bad?"

"Fuck you, it was fucking phenomenal," Xander shoots back, only realizing that Jordan's in the room when the last word leaves his mouth. But hell, he's not about to back down or lie. He holds eye contact for a second, hoping Jordan can see his absolute sincerity. "I'm just pissed I had to get up and see your ugly mugs instead of enjoying the afterglow."

Becks pats him solemnly on the shoulder. "Is hard. You very brave."

The chirping lasts for a little longer, but tapers off when they realize he's not interested in playing any more. It takes him longer to put his finger on the source of his carefully hidden irritation. It's not like Elvis said anything that hasn't been said dozens of times before. But for some reason, this time it bugs him.

It's just dumb, is all. Like, he and Jordan are goddamn professionals, okay. Nobody needs to tell him that they can't be all over each other at the arena. And God knows that if management decided to get rid of one of them, it probably wouldn't be Xander—which isn't his ego talking, it's just facts. So he needs to put on his big boy pants and not be the kind of dick that would get Jordan fired.

But dammit, it rankles. It's dumb that they took separate vehicles to the arena this morning. That everything after they left Jordan's apartment was just, like, classic no-homo behavior. Two bros walking into the arena two feet apart because they're not gay.

Except they totally are—well, Xander's bi, and he's not really sure exactly how Jordan identifies, but so not the point. The point is, last night Xander had Jordan's dick in his mouth and Jordan's hand on his dick and it was phenomenal. And this morning he had Jordan's dick in his ass and that was even better. And they're both fucking adults and fucking professionals, and if Xander wants to touch him casually, kiss him, maybe, maybe pull him into a closet or a storage room to make out if neither of them has anything else to do? He should be fucking able to.

What the fuck exactly is the point of making millions of dollars in the CHL if he has to sneak around like this with his—with his friend?

"Good job today," White says when Xander clomps off the ice at the end of practice. "I don't know what got into you, Richie, but keep it up."

"Sure thing," Xander says, grinning easily and winking at Mac, smile widening at the groan he gets in return. "Planning on it."

12

JORDAN

Standing in the locker room, pinned in place by Xander's gaze, listening to him tell his teammates that they'd had "phenomenal" sex—it's a whole new level of torture. Jordan's face is so hot it feels like it could catch fire at any moment, just explode into flames. He kind of wants the locker room floor to open up and swallow him hole.

But at the same time, he finds himself walking around the arena with a little extra swagger in his step. Because it really was phenomenal. He never thought that he'd be the source of the deets Xander's teammates demand. But since he is, at least he's a really good story.

If he only gets one night, one morning with Xander, at least it was spectacular.

AT LUNCH that day is when it finally hits him. It's the first time he feels really stupid, because staring at the empty chair across the table shouldn't have him feeling like a rock has lodged itself in his chest, heavy and aching. But none of Xander's hookups have been on the team or the crew. He's never gotten to see the aftermath before, and now he's going to get a ringside seat, up close and personal.

It sucks.

Like, sure, the sex was fucking phenomenal. But Jordan finds himself seriously questioning whether a one-and-done—fine, a two-and-done if you count the morning, what the fuck ever—is worth it. He can see the rest of the season stretching out in front of him, no Xander to talk with at lunch or text at random times or watch shows with on the flight. Nothing but casual greetings and torturous massages, but this time he knows what he's missing.

It's really, really going to suck.

He's well on his way to a solid pity party when

Xander drops into the chair across from him, hair still damp from the shower. "Shit, I didn't think Carol was ever gonna stop talking. I'm pretty sure upping my carbs didn't take this much discussion last time." He pauses, looks at Jordan. "Do I have something on my face?"

"Huh?" Jordan has to shake his head to get his brain to reboot. "Uh, no. I was just—thinking about something. Just kind of lost in my head, you know?"

Xander nods his agreement, digging into his own lunch. "Yeah, fair. Anyway, Carol said she's gonna email you, but she wants me bulking, so maybe we need to change up my numbers?"

"I'll talk to Marian," Jordan agrees. It's fucking surreal, sitting across from Xander and talking about their work like—like Xander hadn't been on his knees last night, lashes fluttering against his fucking cheekbones, his mouth an obscene, perfect circle around Jordan's cock.

Jordan shifts uncomfortably in his chair, desperately attempts to redirect his train of thought before he ends up all the way hard here in the arena. "How's your shoulder holding up?"

"Huh," Xander says, like he'd forgotten he had

a shoulder, rolling it absently. "Not bad, honestly. A little tight, but better than preseason for sure. Could still use a massage after, if you have time."

"I think I can manage to fit you in," Jordan says, hoping against hope that it comes out dry instead of fond.

Xander leans forward, lowering his voice, one corner of his mouth tipping up. "Thought that was my line."

Jordan narrowly misses choking on his sandwich. "Jesus fuck, Richards, you can't just say shit like that."

"I just did," Xander retorts, sitting back in his chair, all smug and infuriating. He returns his attention to his lunch, hooking his ankle around Jordan's under the table. Jordan leaves it there until he's finished eating, because he's fucking weak, and he knows it.

Finally, though, he can't stall any longer, pushing back from the table. "Back to work. Come find me when you're ready."

Xander shoots him a lazy salute, scraping the rest of his rice pilaf into a pile on his plate. "Yes, sir," he says with a wink that sends an entirely unprofessional shiver down Jordan's spine.

"Fuck my life," he mutters, turning and heading toward the door. He's pretty sure he hears Xander laughing behind him, but he doesn't turn around to check. Some things he just doesn't need confirmation on.

BY THE TIME Xander shows up in the trainers room, Jordan can't quite believe he hasn't vibrated out of his skin with nerves. He's holding onto composure by the skin of his teeth, because he fucked Xander Richards and now he has to put his hands all over him for his job—it's literally what he gets paid for. How the fuck is this his life anyway?

The only small mercy is that there's nobody else in the trainers room with them, although Jordan's well aware that their solitude is a double-edged sword. Nobody else means that there's no reason for Xander to try and rein in his mouth. Means it's all too easy for Jordan to fantasize, to think "what if?"

What if he left Xander sitting on the edge of the table, went to his knees and sucked his brains out through his cock? What if he got Xander laid out massaging his shoulder, and he begged again, that quiet, almost broken "Please" that shouldn't be nearly as much of a turn-on as it is. What if he bent Xander over the table, got a hand in his hair like he likes and fucked him until he came all over the smooth vinyl surface?

"Fuck," Jordan groans, pressing his fingers against his eyes and doing his best to will his stupid, hopeful erection away. Probably it's never going to happen again. Probably Xander was just flirting, like he always does. Probably he has no intention of fucking Jordan again, getting ready to head on to greener pastures, new and exciting people to fuck. "Fuck me."

"Well, probably not here," Xander says, because of course the asshole picks this exact moment to walk in. "I mean, we could close the door, but if somebody came in, we'd get fined at the very least. I figured you'd want to be professional at work—"

Jordan throws a towel at him, darkly pleased that it hits him dead center in his stupid chest even though his eyes were closed. "Shut the fuck up and get on the table," he growls, unable to keep himself from casting an uneasy glance at the open door.

"Yes, sir," Xander drawls, his voice going low and honey-thick and it's unfair. Life is unfair. "How do you want me?"

"Sit your ass down," Jordan snaps. Goddamnit this is—it's too much. "You know the drill."

Something in his tone must have gotten through to Xander, because he quits the teasing, peels his shirt off quick and efficient and sits down on the table as directed. And his massage is just a massage, because Jordan is a goddamn *professional* who knows his job and he's not going to let Xander reinjure his stupid shoulder because he's fucking around.

And if the rock lodged in Jordan's chest gets a little heavier, a little achier when Xander pulls his shirt back on and leaves with just a nod, well.

Sometimes life is unfair.

It sucks.

JORDAN SETTLES in to do his paperwork, but the back halls of the arena are too quiet, not echoing with the sound of thirty-odd overgrown man-children as usual. It's too quiet to concentrate with the team at one of their innumerable PR opportunities; something about youth field hockey or something. After the third time he gets to the end of a page and realizes he has no idea what he just read, he finally digs his earbuds out of his bag. With the insistent bass beat and Jay-Z's voice in his ears, he's finally able to focus, disappearing into his work.

He has no idea how long it is before the ding of his text notification interrupts the music and pulls him out of the flow of things. He swipes absently at the screen, expecting something from Cammie or Emma, but finds himself freezing in his chair when he sees Xander's name on the lock screen, the notification of a picture message .

Unlocking the phone, he's not sure what he's expecting—honestly, he'd figured the texting would stop, but then, he'd thought that about lunch, too. So maybe Xander wants to still be friends after— well, after. That's fine. Jordan can do that.

He takes a deep breath and opens the text, not sure if he's disappointed or relieved when it's a picture of a wild bunny, poised like it's about to run away, ears up and alert, with a string of heart-eyes emojis to accompany it.

Jordan sends back a string of heart emojis of his own. This is fine. He can do this.

i got so close, Xander sends. *almost touched it*

do you want fleas? because that's how you get fleas, Jordan texts back, smiling despite himself.

whatever your just jealous bc I almost touched a bunny

Jordan rolls his eyes, even though there's no one there to see. Fortunately, the eye-roll emoji is right there. *sure. jealous.*

He gets an emoji with the tongue sticking out in return, and then an, *oops, gtg. Ttyl*

When he puts the phone away and turns back to his paperwork, it takes a minute to realize that he's smiling. He tries to stop, but eventually gives up.

If he's being an idiot and theres no one else around to see, it doesn't count, right?

JORDAN STICKS around the arena as long as he can draw it out, but it's still empty and echoing when he's finished the last bit of neglected paperwork. The rock is back, sharp and sore behind his breastbone, as he makes his way through the bare halls to the exit.

It's stupid to feel lonely at this point. He knows it. It's not even like he's lost Xander as a friend; between the lunch and the teasing and the texting, that much is clear. But for some reason, the idea of heading back to his apartment, being there alone with the memories of last night, this morning—God, he's so stupid. This was the dumbest idea. One of these days he'll learn to think with his actual head instead of his dick.

Making his way out the door, nodding to the security guard, is automatic at this point, his feet carrying him without conscious thought. He's almost all the way to his vehicle, lost in his head, when he notices something different from what he's expecting.

"Hey," Xander says, his tentative voice at odds with his body language, cocky and relaxed as he leans back against Jordan's SUV.

"Hey," Jordan replies. Any other words are just gone, washed out of his head. He's vaguely aware that he's staring, but he can't quite manage to stop. It should be criminal to look as good as Xander does, hands shoved in the pockets of his jeans, the fabric of his t-shirt clinging to his shoulders and chest.

"So I was thinking," Xander says, after a few seconds of silence. "Can I make you dinner?"

Jordan blinks at him, waiting for the punchline. But Xander just stands there, the light of the setting sun turning his hair bright gold at the edges. Before he can stop himself, he blurts out, "Are you going to make me breakfast, too?"

Xander smiles, slow and suggestive in a way that has heat curling in the pit of Jordan's stomach. "I think that can be arranged."

13

XANDER

It's a surprise, honestly, how much Xander is enjoying himself. Walking through the grocery store with Jordan pushing the cart, loading it up with all the ingredients he thinks he'll need for dinner—it's fun.

"Man, I have garlic," Jordan says, rolling his eyes until Xander puts the jar of minced garlic back. "I don't know what kind of useless white boys you usually hook up with, but my kitchen does actually get used for more than frozen pizza and microwave burritos."

"Cool," Xander says, throwing a couple of bunches of asparagus in the cart. "So I don't have to buy a cast-iron skillet?"

He manages to keep a straight face for about

thirty seconds, but Jordan keeps giving him that unimpressed look and eventually he breaks down laughing.

"I swear to God," Jordan mutters, pushing the cart ahead, but Xander saw the way his lips were twitching like he was fighting not to smile.

"C'mon," Xander says, catching up to him. "Steak and then we're done."

Back at Jordan's apartment, that's fun, too. Xander's always liked cooking even for himself. But moving around the kitchen while Jordan sits on a bar stool and sips his beer, watching and commentating while Xander preps the food, it's comfortable in a way he didn't expect.

It's not like Xander's never had sex with the same person twice, okay. Sure, he gets around, but it's not that unusual for him to be coming back for a second, well, third round. And he likes to cook for people; it's been weird since Justin and Brooke left, especially when he finds himself accidentally buying portions for three people instead of one. So this isn't that unusual.

That's what he tells himself while he salts the steaks and sets them aside. While he preheats the oven and wraps the potatoes in foil, chirping back when Jordan tries to give him shit about literally preparing meat and potatoes. While he roasts the asparagus, cooks the steak, and makes Jordan laugh by pretending to plate everything like he's one one of those dumb cooking competition shows.

There's no show to distract them tonight, so Xander carries their plates over to the little table in Jordan's dining nook. He makes his most ostentatious fake bow and intones, "Dinner eez served" in his best snooty accent, which sounds more French-Canadian than anything, but it makes Jordan laugh, so whatever.

It's probably dumb, the little warm glow in the center of his chest, watching Jordan eat food that he made. It's not like it means anything special. He likes cooking for people. He made dinner, they'll fuck again, he'll make breakfast in the morning. Simple.

They start eating mostly in silence—Xander makes a mean steak, if he does say so himself—but then he remembers the story he'd meant to tell Jordan about the tiny little field hockey goalie from today, the way she'd just dive for the ball, not caring if she got a face full of grass and dirt as long as she made the save. And then that reminds Jordan of something from playing youth football, which leads to Xander telling stories from his Mighty Mite days.

The next thing they know, they're sitting there with empty plates, just—talking.

For a second, Xander thinks that maybe this is enough, that it'd be stupid to fuck up what they have when, let's face it, he can get dick literally anywhere. But then Jordan drains his beer, tipping his head back, his throat working as he swallows, and Xander goes hard so suddenly he feels a little light-headed.

"You okay?" Jordan asks, setting the bottle down and licking the last drops of beer from his lips.

Xander does his best not to whimper. "I, uh—yeah." Dammit, he has moves. Where are his moves?

"Let me get the dishes," Jordan says, pushing back from the table and stacking their plates. "Since you cooked and all."

"Okay," Xander replies, deeply, pathetically grateful for the excuse not to stand up at the moment. Not that watching Jordan's ass walk away from him is helping with the situation in his pants even a little bit—"Sorry, what'd you say? I wasn't uh, paying attention."

Jordan smirks back over his shoulder like he knows exactly what Xander was thinking about. "I was asking if you wanted to watch some more Leverage, or something else?"

"Sure." Xander tells himself, firmly, that he doesn't get to be disappointed. If Jordan wants to watch a show, they can watch a fucking show. He's not one of those assholes who thinks dinner entitles him to his date putting out. That's not how shit works. "Yeah, whatever you want."

"Oh yeah?" Jordan straightens up from putting their plates and silverware into the dishwasher, smirk still firmly in place. "So if I said I want to bend you over the bed and fuck you into the mattress instead?"

Xander has to swallow hard, his mouth gone dry. "I—I'd like that. Too. If—If you want."

Jordan cross the distance between them, tugs Xander up and out of his chair, one big hand gently circling his wrist. "Oh, I want. Come on, pretty boy." His grin widens when he notices the reaction Xander can't quite conceal. "Huh. You like it when I tell you you're pretty? I figured you already knew that."

Focusing enough to make a coherent response is difficult; most of his attention is focused on the insistent pressure of his cock against his zipper, the warm grip of Jordan's hand on his skin. Xander just shrugs.

"Nah, none of that," Jordan insists, coming to a stop next to his bed and pulling Xander gently in until they're only inches apart. "How am I supposed to make this good if you don't tell me what you like? C'mon, Richards. Use your words."

"I—" It's hard to focus here, too, now that Jordan's hands have migrated to his waist, thumbs nudging under the hem of his shirt to find skin. "Yeah, I like it. I—uh—you don't have to be, like, gentle. If you don't want to."

Jordan sucks in a breath, his grip tightening for a moment before it relaxes again. "We'll come back to that some other time. But for right now—" he pulls Xander's shirt up and over his head in one quick movement "—you're wearing too many clothes."

"You, too," is all Xander manages to get out before Jordan pulls him in for a kiss, deep and wet and hungry. It feels oddly vulnerable, the soft cotton of Jordan's shirt accentuating his half-naked state, but he kind of likes it, the same shivery feeling in the pit of his stomach as when Jordan called him "pretty boy."

"You first," Jordan rasps when they break apart,

sliding his hands slowly down Xander's chest before unbuttoning his jeans, pulling the zipper slowly down. He doesn't push them down right away, though, instead slipping his hand inside the open fly, cupping his cock and squeezing gently.

The noise that escapes Xander's throat is kind of embarrassing, but all he can do right now is hold on, cling to Jordan's shoulders. Which is flatly ridiculous. They haven't even *started* yet. He still has his pants mostly on, for fuck's sake.

"Yeah," Jordan says, the word a long exhale. The tips of his fingers drag lightly over Xander's cock as his hand moves, thumbs hooking under the waistband of Xander's boxers and pushing them down along with his jeans. "So fucking pretty. I think I changed my mind, though. Want you to ride me."

Xander manages to kick his feet free of his jeans with a reflexive motion, all of his conscious attention focused on watching Jordan peel out of his shirt, strip off his pants and underwear. "Oh—Okay."

Jordan hesitates, one hand on the bedside table drawer. "It's okay if you don't want to. I don't—we don't have to do anything. If you don't want—"

"I want to," Xander interrupts, the words

coming out too loud in his haste. "I really, really want to."

The grin he gets in response is practically blinding. Jordan tosses the lube and a condom onto the bed before climbing onto the mattress, arranging the pillows and settling down with his back against the headboard. "Come on then, pretty boy. Get over here and let me get you ready."

Xander obeys, crossing the empty mattress between them in a graceless scramble that would be slightly embarrassing if he had the brainpower to spare for things like that. But he doesn't, not when he can lean down and kiss Jordan, lick inside his mouth and taste the lingering bitterness of his beer. He arches into the touch of Jordan's hands, sliding firmly down his back, squeezing his ass.

They just make out like that for awhile, naked skin on naked skin. Jordan waits until Xander is grinding helplessly against him, more than half-convinced he can come just like this, with his cock trapped between them. Only then does reach for the lube, flicking it open one-handed and drizzling it over his fingers.

"Ready?" he asks, leaving a string of nipping kisses down the side of Xander's neck.

"Yeah, please." He's perfectly willing to beg at

this point, if that's what he has to do to get Jordan's fingers inside him.

But Jordan doesn't keep him waiting, pressing gently inside where he's still a little loose from this morning. "Okay?" Jordan asks, keeping his movements slow and easy. "Are you sore?"

"I'm a professional hockey player, I'm not gonna break," Xander huffs, pushing back in one sudden movement, doing his best to get Jordan's finger as deep inside him as it'll go. "C'mon, Darling. Another one."

"Whatever you say." Jordan does as he asks, adding another finger.

It's good, it's so good—Xander hisses between his teeth when he rocks his hips back and Jordan's fingertips hit his prostate. "I'm ready," he breathes, grabbing Jordan's shoulders for leverage so he can grind down harder, get Jordan's fingers deeper, even if he's deliberately missing his prostate now. "C'mon, I'm ready."

"One more," Jordan argues, grabbing the lube again and pushing one more finger slowly, relentlessly inside. "You look so fucking pretty like this, did you know that? Can't wait to watch you ride me."

Heat rushes through Xander's face, his body. He

doesn't have to look to know that the flush has spread down his neck, across his chest, but that doesn't matter right now. He reaches down to grab the forgotten condom packet, whimpering a little at the change in angle. He rips the packet open and reaches down to roll it onto Jordan's cock.

"I'm ready," he insists, rising up on his knees and lining himself up. Jordan withdraws his fingers slowly, but doesn't protest, sucking in a long breath when Xander starts to sink down onto his cock.

Xander lowers himself slowly, thighs and abs aching with the strain, savoring the hot, thick slide, the feeling of fullness. He wants to close his eyes, to feel the sensations even more intensely, but he also wants to watch Jordan's face. His eyes are downcast, watching the place where his cock disappears inside Xander, teeth digging into his lower lip.

Having Jordan's attention laser-focused on him like that is almost as overwhelming as the purely physical sensations. Especially when his gaze drags up Xander's body like a nearly physical caress, his hands flexing on Xander's waist.

"So fucking pretty," he repeats, his voice a low rasp. He drags his hands slowly down over Xander's thighs, then back up again. Up his chest, thumbs dragging gently over his nipples, smiling when he shivers. "Could watch you all fucking day."

They both groan when Xander settles all the way down, fitting into the cradle of Jordan's hips without any space between them. He pauses there for a minute, hesitating before leaning in, just a little closer, asking without words for what he wants.

Jordan meets him halfway, big hands coming up to cradle his face and angle it just so, devouring his mouth hungrily. Xander gets lost in it a little, but his hips have other ideas, moving without his conscious input. They break apart, both breathing hard, as he does it again, lifting up further this time.

"Come on," Jordan says, stroking his hands down Xander's back, curving them over his ass. "Let's see that pro hockey player cardio endurance."

Xander rolls his eyes a little at the chirp, but it helps dull the shivery intensity of Jordan's eyes on him. "Okay, you asked for it."

He braces himself on Jordan's shoulders and starts to move in earnest, lifting and lowering himself, biting his lip. It feels like sparks dancing across his skin, lighting him up until every inch is sensitized, alert to the slightest touch. "Fuck," he groans, throwing his head back. "Fuck, please—"

"What do you need?" Jordan asks, thrusting up just enough to force a whine out of his throat. "C'mon, tell me. Whatever you need."

"Touch me," Xander begs, too far gone to care how need, how lost he sounds. "Please, I'm so close—"

Jordan's hand is curled around his cock before he can even finish the sentence. "Shh, I've got you. So fucking gorgeous, Xander. You gonna come for me?"

He can't find the words to reply. Jordan's hand on his cock is like closing a circuit. He's focused on the desperate, driving need to come, his attention narrowed down to the slide of Jordan's cock inside him as he rises and falls, fucking himself down onto Jordan's cock and then up into Jordan's hand.

"That's it," Jordan murmurs, wrapping his other arm around Xander's back. "Come on, come for me. So fucking pretty when you come—"

Xander loses the rest of his words, pulse pounding in his ears as he comes, his whole body shaking with the force of it. When he can pay attention to his body again, he's wrapped in Jordan's arms, face buried in his neck, held close as Jordan thrusts up into him one last time before going still.

The silence that follows is almost more intimate

than the sex. He can't tell where his heartbeat ends and Jordan's begins, both of them hammering where their chests are pressed together. It's hot and sticky and a little uncomfortable.

He never wants to move.

"—AND Jordan still won't let me go up on my bench even though I did 260 no problem—" Xander breaks off mid-sentence when he registers the look Justin is giving him. "What?"

"Nothing," Justin says with a shrug and the innocent face that hasn't fooled Xander even once. "Go on."

Xander snorts. "I know you and that's not nothing. Spit it the fuck out already."

"Do you even have any idea how many times you've mentioned Jordy?"

It's Xander's turn to shrug. "What, are you counting?"

"Well, I wasn't," Justin drawls. "But then you decided to spend five minutes raving about his massages, and another ten about his cooking—"

"It's a nice break from chicken and broccoli," Xander retorts, doing his best to ignore the heat creeping across his cheeks. "Besides, you and your wife were the ones who told me to go out and make a friend. Well, I did it, I made a friend. I figured you'd be happy."

Justin's smirk softens into something more real. "I am happy, bro. You know you have a tendency to go all hermit. I'm just a little surprised, is all."

Xander rolls his eyes. "I have had friends other than you, you know. I'm not completely incompetent at normal human interaction."

"I know," Justin agrees. "But you don't usually make the effort. I'm glad you did, though. It seems like Jordy's a really cool dude. I'm glad you've got him. And I'm not going to ask how you know about his shower—"

"I—he—" Xander sputters, unprepared for the sudden conversational turn.

Justin lifts a hand. "I said I wasn't going to ask. Just try not to fuck it up, eh?"

"Whatever." Xander casts about frantically for a change of subject. "Where's your better half, anyway?"

"She's got some thing with the other SOPs," Justin answers, with a look that says he knows what Xander's doing but isn't going to call him on it. This time, anyway. "But let's talk about that game against New Mexico. That pass was fucking *filthy*, dude. I thought the puck was gonna go right by Sasha—"

Xander laughs. "Yeah, so did he. We had to hear about it at least twenty times in the bar that night."

"Like you weren't just as bad," Justin teases.

"You take that back," Xander demands, doing his best to focus on the conversation and not on the little voice in the back of his head that says Justin's right, that he's going to fuck it up.

It's not just the sex, although that honestly keeps getting better, every time more mind-blowing than the last—sometimes literally, like the time he actually got the nerve to pull Jordan into a supply closet and blow him. But they're still doing all the stuff they were doing before they started fucking. Still eating lunch together, still texting each other about books and TV shows and memes they saw on Twitter or other random shit.

They're still friends. He's not quite sure how that happened, but he's sure as hell not going to question it.

Maybe if he doesn't think about it too much, he can keep from fucking it up.

Maybe.

14

JORDAN

"Hey," Cammie says when he gets close enough to the table that she doesn't have to yell. "I wasn't sure if you were gonna make it."

Jordan shrugs out of his coat, slipping into the last empty chair and picking up his menu. "You know how it is once the season gets going."

"Or when you've got a new boyfriend," Emma sing-songs, grinning when everyone else starts laughing.

"I don't have a boyfriend," Jordan says, doing his best to keep his voice level.

Matt shakes his head. "Nah, man, it's okay. You can tell us. It's been, like, a month since the last time we saw you."

"More," Dan corrects. "He came to game night in October, but we haven't seen him since then. And he spent the whole night texting somebody, but he wouldn't tell us who."

Jordan does his best to ignore them, scanning the menu to try and decide on his entree. "What?" he snaps, finally looking up when Cammie pokes him in the side.

"Look, I'm sorry," she says. "You don't have to talk about it if you don't want to."

"Nothing to talk about," he replies, keeping his tone carefully casual. "I mean, I'd love a boyfriend, but I don't have one. And if I did, I don't know if I'd have time for him, since I haven't even seen you guys in over a month. What's going on with you?"

He listens with half an ear to Emma's problems with her boss and unsuccessful attempts to find a new job, Cammie's new podcast idea, and, when Matt excuses himself to the bathroom, Dan's plans to propose on their anniversary. Nobody seems to notice anything insincere in his congratulations, but he hates himself a little for how his first reaction was jealousy, not to be happy for his friends.

Between that and the uncomfortable feeling that he's not telling them the entire truth, he's slightly uncomfortable for the entire dinner. It's not that he doesn't want to tell them about Xander. But what is there to tell, honestly? They go to work and hang out, they come home and hang out, sometimes they fuck.

They never talk about it.

They're not dating.

It's kind of the worst, Jordan thinks morosely, stabbing at his asparagus as the conversation flows around him. He should cut it off, should tell Xander to go find another fuckbuddy, should start trying to find someone who actually wants to be in a relationship and isn't an emotionally stunted professional athlete.

Not that this is Xander's fault. Right from the beginning, he was absolutely clear about who he was and what he was looking for.

No, it's Jordan's fault. Because he knows what he should do, and instead he keeps coming back for whatever crumbs of attention Xander will give him. Keeps thinking that it means something, when Xander curls into him, touches him randomly. When he spends time with him, seems happy to do so.

He forces himself to shove those thoughts to the back of his head, to pay attention to his friends instead of wallowing in his feelings. And he actually succeeds, for awhile. Until they're sitting around the table, debating dessert, and his phone vibrates in his pocket.

It's Xander, of fucking course. *wanna come over when ur done?*

Jordan stares at his loc kscreen for a moment before putting the phone away and weighing in on the pro-dessert side of the discussion. They eventually end up ordering a mascarpone cheesecake and a brownie to split, rearranging seats once they arrive so everyone can get a bite of the one they wanted.

Once the checks are signed, they spill out into the night, still talking, lingering in the parking garage until the already-cold temperatures drive them into their vehicles. Jordan fastens his seatbelt, starts the engine, but pulls his phone out instead of putting the SUV into gear.

yeah, I'm omw, he texts, then puts his phone away and backs out of his parking space.

It's stupid. He knows it's stupid.

He just doesn't care.

"HEY." Xander smiles as he opens the door wearing only a pair of low-slung sweatpants, as fucking usual when he's lying around the house. He grabs two handful of the front of Jordan's shirt, pulling him inside. Like he's eager. Like he wants this. "Wasn't sure if you were gonna make it."

Jordan can't think of anything to say that doesn't sound super pissed and bitchy and, well, boyfriendy. And that's not what they are. So he gets his hands on Xander instead, right above the waistband of his sweatpants and pulls him in for a kiss.

The kiss is maybe a little rougher than Jordan was planning, but Xander melts into it, opening for him like he wants nothing else. When Jordan lifts his head, Xander's pupils are wide and dark, his mouth wet and red.

"I don't want to be gentle," Jordan says, not sure if he's warning himself or Xander.

It doesn't seem to matter, though. Xander's cock twitches where it's pressed against Jordan's thigh, and he looks like someone told him the Wendigos made the playoffs. "I—that's cool," he says, his voice a little choked-sounding. "I like that. Too."

"Yeah?" Jordan fists a a hand in his hair. The slightest downward pressure has Xander folding gracefully to his knees, looking up at Jordan from other his lashes.

"Yeah," he confirms, hands resting on his thighs, erection tenting his sweatpants.

Ordinarily he'd already have Jordan's jeans halfway to his knees by this point, hands all over him. It takes Jordan a minute to realize that he's waiting for permission.

"Fuck," Jordan groans, lifting his other hand to cradle Xander's face, running a thumb over his lips.

Xander's eyes flutter closed as he parts his lips, sucking Jordan's thumb inside and curling his tongue around it when he can't take it any deeper.

"Look at you," Jordan marvels, pulling his thumb free and popping open the button on his jeans before digging out the condom packet from his pocket. "I'm gonna fuck your mouth first, and then I'm gonna bend you over your bed."

He half expects a protest, or at least some sort of verbal response, but Xander just nods and lets his mouth fall open a little more. Waiting.

Jordan shudders. Getting his cock out one-handed is a little awkward, but he manages eventually, pushing his boxer briefs down just far enough to let it spring free. Putting the condom on is a little easier, more habitual. Xander makes a small noise, licks his lips, but stays where he is until Jordan uses the grip on his hair to guide him forward, to thrust into the lush, wet heat of his mouth.

It's tempting, so tempting, just to come like this, fucking into Xander's mouth. He's already embarrassingly close, just from this. But a quick and dirty orgasm isn't going to be enough to soothe the restless irritation, the *want* bubbling under his skin. No matter how many times they do this, it never eases. He always wants more.

"Bedroom," he orders, tugging on Xander's hair until he pulls back with a protesting noise. "The floor's hell on your knees. Come on."

Xander allows himself to be pulled to his feet, guided toward his bedroom. Jordan takes deep, even breaths as they walk. No matter what Xander says, he's not going to rush the prep, not going to risk hurting him. Even if part of him wants to just push Xander down onto the bed and *take*, stake his claim, even if only to himself.

To believe, just this once, that Xander can be his.

He pushes, one hand between Xander's shoulder blades, bending him down over the bed. He looks like porn, his sweats barely clinging to the swell of his ass, the soft fabric draping over the curves of it. Jordan takes a minute, lets himself anticipate, before hooking his fingers under the waistband and pulling the sweats down.

He freezes when he sees the base of the butt plug nestled between Xander's cheeks.

"Surprise," Xander says, sounding almost shy. "I had a little time before you got here, so—"

He shivers as Jordan reaches out, running his fingers around the base. It's glass, cool to the touch where it's not resting against skin, swirled with decorative colors. It looks deceptively pretty, almost delicate.

"How long?" Jordan almost doesn't recognize his voice, hoarse and hungry. "How long have you had it in?"

Xander shrugs. "Maybe forty-five minutes. You can take it out and just slide right—"

He cuts off as Jordan pulls the plug out a fraction of an inch, pushes it back in. "Or I could just do this," Jordan muses. He angles the toy just a little bit, smiling when Xander's whole body shakes on the next thrust. "Fuck you with this toy until you come all over yourself. Think you could do that? Come just from this plug in your ass?"

"I—fuck—I don't know!" Xander nearly wails when Jordan hits his prostate again.

"Is that good?" Jordan asks, timing his next thrust for when Xander opens his mouth to answer.

He gets a broken moan in response. "Not—Jesus fuck—not as good—as your cock—" Xander pants, his knuckles white where he grips the sheet. "Come on, Jordy, *please*—"

"Please, what?" Jordan has no idea how he's keeping his tone calm, even, when it feels like he's hanging onto control by his fingernails. But as worked up as he is, as much as he wants to pull the plug out and replace it with his aching cock, something about this has him feeling more settled, more secure than he has in days.

"Please," Xander chokes out, grinding down against the mattress like he's desperate for friction against his cock. "Fuck me, please, *please*—"

Jordan pulls the plug out again, but instead of pushing it back in this time, he keeps going, drawing it slowly out. He watches in fascination as Xander's rim stretches around the widest part of the toy, pausing with it there and reaching down to touch.

"Fuck." Xander can't seem to stop moving as the plug finally slips out, his body rolling, ass thrusting back like he's trying to get it back inside. "Fuck, fuck, come *on*, I'm ready—"

Jordan thinks about teasing more, about pushing his fingers inside, just to check, but he's drawn this out long enough. He doesn't even want to take the time to shed his shirt or his jeans. So he lets himself do what they both want, lines his cock up and thrusts inside in one fast, brutal snap of his hips.

"Fuck yes!" Xander tries to push back into him, but Jordan gets a hand on the small of his back, pinning him to the bed. "Yeah, Jordy, just like that, fuck me, please—"

"Like that?" Jordan growls, doing it again. "That what you want?"

Xander moans, going pliant under his hands. Even though Jordan knows he's perfectly capable of getting free if he wants, it's still a heady feeling. "Yeah, fuck, right there. Please—"

"You're gonna come like this," Jordan tells him, setting a fast, hard pace. "With me holding you down and fucking you. I'm not even gonna touch your cock and you're still gonna come. Aren't you?"

"I—fuck." Xander whimpers, shaking under Jordan's hands. "I don't—don't know if can—"

"You will," Jordan tells him. "You always come for me when I tell you to. You're gonna do it this time, too."

Xander's breathing like he's just skated a 20-minute shift and he practically wails when Jordan leans forward a little, catches his prostate on the next thrust. "Fuck, fuck, fuck!"

"That's it." Jordan babbles, no longer able to spare any attention for the words coming out of his mouth. Every bit of focus he has left is aimed at making Xander come before he does. "You can do this for me, always so good for me. That's it, that's good. You close?"

"Please," Xander begs, his voice hoarse and rasping. "Please, so close, please, Jordy, fuck me—"

Jordan bites his lip, his chest heaving as he tries to keep up the pace. "Come on, come for me, baby—"

He snaps his mouth shut as soon as he realizes what he's said, but Xander's upper body is already arching up off the bed as he comes. His ass tightens around Jordan's cock, dragging his orgasm relentlessly out of him.

When he comes back to awareness of his body, his hands are braced on the mattress on either side of Xander's head, his heart thundering in his chest. "Sorry," he mutters, pulling back. "I'll get off you. Gimme a sec."

"Take your time," Xander mumbles into the

sheet. "I'm not getting up for at least a year."

Jordan eventually manages to get up and dispose of the condom. It's only as he's washing his hands in the bathroom, staring blankly at his reflection in the mirror, that he remembers the last thing he'd said. The endearment that had fallen from his lips so easily, like—fuck, like he meant it.

He's terrifyingly sure that he did mean it.

The bright side to not having fully undressed—he shudders a little at the thought of how fucking hot that had been, fucking Xander like that, like they were both too desperate for him to get out of his clothes—is that all he has to do is tuck his cock back in his pants, zip them back up. Aside from the traces of sweat at his hairline, the desperation in his eyes—it's like nothing ever happened.

Xander barely stirs when he comes back into the bedroom, only lifting his head when Jordan crosses to the other door. "Wha—are you going?"

Jordan shrugs, doing his best to be casual. "Yeah, I've got some stuff. I'll see you at the arena tomorrow."

"Okay," Xander says, blinking slowly. "I'll —see you."

Every step down the hallway toward the front door feels like it takes an eternity.

15

XANDER

Ever since the night—the incredibly, mind-blowingly hot night—that Jordan had bent him over his bed and fucked his brains out, things have been weird. There's nothing super specific Xander can put his finger on, nothing he can point to. They still eat lunch, they still text. Jordan keeps his massages scrupulously professional in the trainers' room and not so professional if they're at Xander's house, or Jordan's apartment.

They have lots of sex. Xander plays lots of hockey. The Wendigos are winning more than they're losing. On the surface everything is great.

He can't shake the feeling that something is wrong.

"Everything cool with you?" he asks over lunch one day.

Jordan blinks at him from across the table. "Uh, yeah? Coach White actually said I'm probably getting a raise this year."

"Cool," Xander replies, trying not to sigh. "You deserve it."

And if he gets a little distracted by the way Jordan looks shyly down at his plate, well, he's only human

He tries again later that night, while they're waiting for the next episode of Stranger Things to load. "So is everything—"

Before he gets any further, he's cut off by Jordan's ringtone. "Shit, I've gotta take this. Hey, Nana," he says, lifting the phone to his ear. "Huh? No, just watching TV with a friend."

Xander pauses the episode when it finally loads, pulling out his own phone to get a few pages of reading done. He's honestly trying not to eavesdrop, but Jordan's right there in the dining area.

So it's not hard to hear, "No, Nana. No, I've told you, it's hard to date during the season. Yeah, I'd like a boyfriend but—no. No one like that." A pause. "No, I already went on a date with your dentist's son, remember, he spent the whole time texting his ex." Another pause. "I know. Yeah, of course—you know I do. Someday. I've got time."

He laughs. "Yes, I promise. Lots of grandkids, someday. So many that you get tired of 'em. Yeah, I love you too."

Jordan doesn't return the couch as soon as he hangs up. Xander can see him out of the corner of his eye, staring out the window for long minutes before going into the kitchen, opening and closing cabinets, then the fridge. Finally he comes back to the couch with two beers, offering one to Xander without speaking.

Xander wants to ask—it's actually surprising how much he wants to ask—but he can take a hint. Maybe Jordan doesn't know what's bugging him, maybe he's just not ready to talk about it, but either way, it's not Xander's place to push. That's not what they do, who they are.

They're not boyfriends.

So he accepts the beer and pretends he doesn't notice the tightness in Jordan's shoulders, the way he holds himself separate instead of leaning into Xander the way he usually does.

"Fuck," Xander mumbles, catching himself as he trips coming down the stairs from the plane. He doesn't realize that it's Jordan's shoulder he's caught himself on for a few seconds, still half-asleep. "Sorry, Jordy."

"No worries," Jordan says, his voice cracking on a yawn halfway through the second word. "Long fuckin' flight from Albuquerque."

Xander nods, also yawning. "Yeah. I'm wiped."

"Everybody is," Jordan agrees, falling into step with him as they head toward the parking shuttle.

Under ordinary circumstances, he'd be able to muster up at least a flicker of arousal at the way they keep bumping into each other, the arm Jordan loops around his shoulders to help keep him upright. But right now all he can think about is a horizontal surface and sleep, curled up around Jordan.

"Hey," he says softly once the rest of the team and staff are dispersing through the parking structure. "Come back to mine?"

Jordan blinks at him slowly. "No offense, but I don't think I could get it up with a crane right now."

"Fuck, me either," Xander agrees, hitching the

strap of his duffel bag higher on his shoulder. "Not after three away games. Just sleep, promise."

He waits, swaying slightly on his feet, until Jordan shrugs. "Fine, but you ride with me. I don't trust you behind the wheel right now. We can come back for your truck tomorrow."

"Cool." Xander follows to where Jordan's SUV is parked, climbing into the passenger side and buckling his seatbelt before reclining the seat all the way back. Jordan starts the engine—

—and the next thing Xander knows, he's being shaken awake.

"C'mon, sleeping beauty, we're here," Jordan says, one corner of his mouth tipping upward.

Keeping his eyes open is actually painful, so once they're inside the house Xander doesn't bother. He drops his duffel inside the front door, kicking off his shoes. Stripping out of his clothes one piece at a time as he stumbles down the hall-way, he leaves them where they land, crawling into his bed with the last of his energy.

He's only barely aware of the mattress moving as Jordan joins him, just enough to shift over and throw an arm and a leg over him before sinking into sleep.

THE ROOM IS bright but his eyes still feel like they weigh a thousand pounds each, so Xander doesn't bother opening them. His alarm hasn't gone off yet, so there's no need to get up. He can stay right here, his head pillowed on Jordan's shoulder, Jordan's heart beating slowly and steadily under his hand.

He drifts in that hazy, half-asleep place for awhile. Maybe he goes back to sleep for awhile. But eventually his bladder's demands make themselves known, urgently enough that he can't ignore them any longer. So he forces his eyes open, doing his best to slide out of the bed without waking Jordan.

For a minute when Jordan stirs, mumbling something under his breath, he thinks he's fucked it up, but Jordan just rolls onto his side, burrowing his face into the pillow with a grumbling noise.

Xander stumbles to the bathroom as quietly as he can manage, suppressing a groan of relief as he empties his bladder. He gives his hands a cursory wash before returning to the bedroom and slipping under the covers, biological pressures eased.

Jordan sleeps through it all, his face peaceful in the morning light. Xander wants to slip back into sleep, but he doesn't get to just look at Jordan very often. They're always at the arena, filled with people who'll chirp him if they catch him staring. Or if they're alone, they're doing something—watching a show, or reading, or fucking. Always something.

He thinks vaguely about waking Jordan up for lazy morning sex, but honestly his side still aches from the check he took in their game against the Jackalopes. He's too tired to be more than half-hard now that the pressure on his bladder is relieved. So he lies there, warm and comfortable and still half-asleep, dreamily wondering how he's never noticed before that Jordan's lashes are long enough to rest on his cheekbones, slightly curled at the ends.

I could wake up like this every morning, he thinks, absently, before the shock of it jolts him fully awake, adrenaline sizzling down his spine like lightning.

Somehow he manages to make it out of bed without waking Jordan. His sweatpants are on the floor next to the bed, so he slips them on, padding out into the hallway in his sock feet. He finds his t-shirt caught on the coat closet doorknob and his jacket on the back of the coach. Shoving his feet into his trainers, he hesitates for a moment beside the front door.

Finally, he scrawls *Gone to get groceries—back*

soon on a spare scrap of paper and leaves it next to the coffeemaker, where Jordan will see it if he wakes up alone.

It's not a lie if he runs to the grocery store. A couple of miles are just what he needs to work this panic out from under his skin. Because this—this is not what Jordan signed on for. This is not what they're doing. Yeah, Jordan wants a relationship, a boyfriend. But he deserves someone better. Someone who's actually capable of giving him what he needs. Of loving him. Someone who isn't fundamentally broken.

Xander runs a little faster, pushes himself a little harder. He's going to have to end things, to let Jordan find the kind of person he wants. He's not going to be the kind of selfish dick that holds his friend back from a chance at happiness.

The two miles pass in a blur. He only realizes when he's standing outside the doors of the supermarket that he's managed to leave the house without his wallet.

He takes the long way home.

16

JORDAN

When Jordan wakes up, the light is filtering around the edges of the shades, warm and golden. The windows are on the wrong side of the bed, though; it takes him a minute to remember the events of last night. Loading onto the plane at one in the morning, not landing in Milwaukee until almost four. Xander's sleepy-eyed request that had been impossible to ignore, to deny, with his defenses so low.

In that moment, he's almost grateful that Xander isn't there on the bed next to him. Jordan rolls onto his stomach and buries his face in the pillow, stifling a groan. He's so fucking stupid. Bad enough to have a crush on Xander Richards, possibly the most notorious player in the CHL.

Questionable to make friends with him, start hanging out with him—although Jordan hasn't ever been able to resist someone who genuinely needs a friend, not even back in kindergarten when Mandy Lewis would sit by herself instead of playing with everyone else.

But this—

Jordan screams, very softly, into the pillow. He's such a fucking idiot, he had to go and fall in love with Xander. Even if falling in love with your fuck-buddy wasn't one of the classic blunders, falling for Xander definitely qualifies.

And of course he couldn't have this realization when he's safely in his own home. No, he has to be in Xander's bed, where the sheets smell like his dumb salon shampoo and the cheap deodorant he buys in bulk. Where Xander is probably cooking breakfast in the kitchen, because he's the perfect boyfriend in every way, except for the part where he's not actually Jordan's boyfriend.

He peeks at the clock on the bedside table and allows himself five minutes. Five minutes of wallowing before he gets up, pulls on his big boy pants, and deals with this.

But after he takes care of business in the bathroom, pulling on his discarded clothes and heading out to the living area, he finds—nothing. No Xander, no breakfast, just an empty kitchen and a note by the coffeemaker that says Xander went for groceries.

Jordan's not exactly proud of how fast he sneaks out, pausing only long enough to text Xander —*going home for clean clothes*—but sometimes you have to do things if you want to survive. He'll figure out how he's going to get himself out of this mess later.

Right now, he just needs to go.

HE DOESN'T REMEMBER that he drove both of them, leaving Xander's truck at the airport, until he's home and standing in the shower. "Fuck," he says, banging his head lightly against the tile wall. "Fuck my fucking life."

He lingers under the spray until the water starts to cool, finally forcing himself to turn it off and step out onto the rug. Drying off is something that can take awhile, if he makes sure to meticulously dry every inch of his skin. And then he has to find clean clothes, which is a bit of an adventure, since he hasn't had time to do laundry in over a week. Then he needs coffee, and breakfast.

But finally he can't delay looking at his phone any longer. He's not sure if he's relieved or pissed that there's no reply to his text, but he's not going to leave Xander stranded. That's not cool. So he mentally fortifies himself and types *lmk when you're ready to go get your truck*

The little typing animation pops up almost immediately. *No worries, grabbed a lyft. See you at the barn*

Jordan stares at his phone and gives serious consideration to calling in sick. But after that long stretch of away games, they're going to have so many players who need a massage, either before or after the optional skate. And leaving Marian to deal with the training alone is a dick move, one he'll end up paying for. So he tucks his phone in his pocket, grabs his coat and his keys, and heads out the door to do his job. Because he may be—okay, he absolutely is—a fucking idiot who fell in love with Xander Richards, but he's also a goddamn professional.

He makes it to the arena and the trainers room without incident. It's stupid to be surprised that Xander doesn't appear with a coffee, but somehow he still is. It's stupid to check his phone a zillion times per hour to see if Xander's texted—he hasn't—but Jordan does it. It's stupid to feel saddened by the empty chair across from him at lunch, so he gets mad instead, tearing through his lunch in half the time he usually takes.

Anger carries him through the rest of the day, massaging overworked muscles and bodies strained by problematic joints. He doesn't realize until Marian pokes her head in on the way out, her eyes worried as she gently chirps him, that he was waiting for Xander.

It's stupid. He's stupid. But he can feel the Xander-shaped hole next to him for the entire drive home.

BY THE TIME he unlocks his apartment and steps inside, he's angry again. Because really? Fuck Xander Richards. Where does he get off? Maybe it was all a ploy. Maybe he just couldn't stand not getting what he wanted, so he decided to date Jordan without really dating him. Pretend to be friends, to like books and TV shows.

And he fell for it, like the dumbass romantic he

is, Jordan thinks, pulling out a skillet to cook his dinner and banging the cabinet door closed with enough force to bounce it open again. Fell, yet again, for the hot guy who has absolutely no interest in dating him. It's not like he doesn't know what Xander's like. It's not like he hasn't seen the parade of people into and out of Xander's bed, even in less than three years with the team. He *knew*. He knew and he still walked right into the trap. Let himself believe that the cuddles and the kisses and the lunch dates meant something. Something more than Xander wanting to get his dick wet.

He wants to call someone, to vent this anger bubbling up inside him before it explodes and tears him apart. Not his Nana—Jesus, he'd never hear the end of it if he tried to explain to his Nana that he fucked up and grew feelings for his fuckbuddy. She'd be on the next flight out of Baton Rouge just to kick his dumb ass. He could call Cammie, or Emma, they'd be sympathetic. But their solution is a hundred percent going to involve setting him up with someone, or several someones, and that—he's not ready for that. Not yet.

The cherry on top of this stupid shit sundae is that the person he wants to call is Xander. But you can't exactly bitch about your broken heart to the dude who broke it in the first place. Who warned you of exactly what he was before this whole thing started. Can you?

Jordan stares at the skillet for a long, long minute, then puts it back Into the cabinet. His keys are still in his pocket, coat hanging on a hook by the door. He shoves his feet into his shoes, cursing when the tongue of the right one gets balled up under his toes and he has to pull it off and put it back on again.

Fuck this suffering in silence shit. It takes two to fuck, and Xander's been right with him the whole time. It's time he got a piece of Jordan's mind.

17
—————

XANDER

By the time he gets home, hours earlier than usual because he snuck out of the arena like a coward instead of getting his usual massage, Xander is fucking miserable. Not just physically, although his shoulder complains with every breath despite the ice pack he's applied and his quads are entertaining themselves by attempting to drop him on his ass if he walks too fast.

But the physical discomfort is something he's accustomed to, something he's learned to live with, to ignore as much as possible. And he knows, with a bleak certainty, that it's only going to get worse as he gets older. He's got another five, maybe seven years of good play left in him, at the outside. If he doesn't take a puck to the head or a bad check or any of a thousand other ways he could go out. But he's been playing hockey for almost as long as he's been alive; pain and discomfort are just another part of the game.

No, it's not the physical misery that's getting to him. He hasn't talked to Jordan all day, and it's like an itch under his skin, one he just can't scratch. He has no fucking idea how Jordan got so entwined in his life. And now he's pining like a smitten rookie, just because he didn't bring Jordan his morning coffee. Didn't eat lunch with him, or text him. Didn't lie down on the massage table and let his hands work their magic.

It's the right decision. He knows it is. Jordan deserves everything. Deserves somebody who can love him. And Xander knows himself. Knows that he's weak and selfish. If he doesn't cut things off completely, he's going to cave. He'll keep taking and taking until Jordan pushes him away, or until he has nothing left to give.

So this total break, as much as it sucks, is necessary. But Xander can't fucking settle, moving from the couch to the kitchen to his bedroom and back again. His house is big, sure. Not as big as some of the other guys' houses, but plenty big for one person. It's never felt this empty before, though, not even when Justin and Brooke packed up and moved to Seattle. Empty and quiet, his footsteps echoing off the walls.

He forces himself to stop and reheat one of the meals in his freezer; there's no way he's going to be able to focus enough to cook something. His body needs fuel, needs to replace what he used up, so he chews and swallows his way through the food mechanically, only realizing when he's done that he has no idea what it was. The reusable container goes into the dishwasher and he pops the top off a beer, taking it to the couch.

As usual, despite having over 500 channels, there's nothing on to catch his attention. After flipping through the complete lineup at least twice, Xander settles on Sportscenter, letting the announcers' conversations wash over him without really paying attention.

HE'S DOZING on the couch, drifting fitfully in and out of wakefulness, when his Skype ringtone startles him awake. Fumbling his phone off his chest and almost dropping it in the process, he finally manages to answer the call.

"Bro!" Justin narrows his eyes. "You look like shit."

"Thanks," Xander says dryly. "Just what I love to hear."

Justin rolls his eyes. "Seriously though, I know you guys just came off a long-ass roadie, but I figured you'd gotten some sleep by now.

"I did. And I was getting more when somebody called me."

"Nobody forced you to answer." Justin eyes him closely for a minute. "Okay, so you've slept, today was optional skate so you could take it easy. What gives? Why're you lying there looking like someone ran over your cat?"

Xander sighs. "I don't have a cat. I'm allergic to cats, a fact I know you're aware of."

"Quit changing the subject," Justin orders, "or I'll go get Brooke."

"Fine." Xander chews on his lower lip, trying to figure out how to explain things. "So, like, we got home from the roadie at like 4, right? I'm dead on my fucking feet, so Jordy tells me he'll drive me home because he doesn't trust me to drive like that."

Justin nods. "He's a good dude."

Xander has to close his eyes for a second against the wave of renewed guilt. "Yeah. Anyway, I just—"

They sit in silence for awhile while Xander struggles to find words. "I just realized, I'm kind of fucking him over? Like, he's spending time with me and shit, but he wants—he deserves—I heard him on the phone with his Nana the other night. He wants a boyfriend. How's he gonna get one if he's hanging out with me all the time?"

"He's a grown-ass man," Justin responds, his forehead furrowed. "You're not like, chaining him to your couch and forcing him to watch Leverage with you. He can go on dates and shit if he wants."

"Yeah, but—" Xander hesitates. "He won't, though. Not while we're fucking."

Justin freezes for a moment, then shakes his head. "Xan—bro—"

"I know! I know!" Xander groans. "And he—he deserves better than my fickle ass. So I just kind of —ghosted him, today. But it sucks. I miss talking to him."

When he dares to look back at the screen, Justin is grinning at him.

"What the fuck are you so happy about?" Xander growls

"You're in love with him, you dumbass."

Xander can practically hear the needle scratch in his brain. "I—what—no. No, I don't—I'm not—"

"You totally are," Justin crows. "You talk about him all the fucking time, you're miserable because you didn't get to see him today, you keep talking about how he deserves better. You're in love with him."

"I don't—I don't do that. I just—I can't." Xander's heart is racing. "I've tried, Justin, you have no idea how many times I've tried. But I've only— there's something wrong with me. I can't—I can't."

Justin's smile fades into something more like his *that's okay, buddy, we'll get 'em next time* face. "Hold on."

He's gone before Xander can protest. Not that he's capable of it, at the moment. He sits there, staring blankly at the screen and Justin's empty desk chair. Justin is wrong. He's just—he's wrong. It's not possible. It's—he can't be.

Between one blink and the next, Brooke is sitting in the chair. "Hey, Xan," she says gently. "Justin's not in here right now, but he told me what you said."

"I can't," he says, the only words he can get out. "I just—I can't."

"Oh, honey." She sighs. "Have you ever heard the word 'demiromantic'? Or 'aromantic'?"

Xander blinks at her, trying to parse the subject change. "No?"

"Aromantic people don't usually experience romantic attraction. They have friendships and other close relationships, but they don't need a romantic relationship in their life, they don't fall in love the way other people think of it."

"Okay," Xander says slowly, his mind spinning. "There's a word—there are other people like that?"

Brooke nods. "Lots of them. And then there are demiromantic people. They only experience romantic attraction, wanting to be in a romantic relationship with someone, after they've already had a very close friendship with them. Sound familiar?"

It's like the ground shifting under his feet, shaking up everything he thought he knew about himself. Xander grabs onto the back of the couch with his free hand, waiting for things to settle. "So, like—like me. With my feelings for—for—"

"For Justin," she finishes for him when it's clear he can't. "And now, it sounds like, for Jordan. What is it with you and J names, Xan?"

"Shut up," he responds reflexively. "Are—do you think? Really?"

She smiles. "What was the thing that really freaked you out, that you didn't want to tell Justin about?"

"I woke up," Xander says haltingly, tripping over his words. "And he was still sleeping, and I thought—I thought that I wanted to wake up like that, every morning. With him there."

"And then you ghosted him, because?"

Xander swallows. "Because I know he wants a real relationship, with somebody who loves him. And he—he deserves that."

"Sounds like love to me," she says softly. "Can I let Justin back in now?"

"Yeah," he says, clearing his throat when his voice cracks. "Yeah, go ahead."

She turns and looks to her right, but the sound of the door opening comes before she can even say anything. Justin bounds into the frame, draping himself over her shoulders. For once, it doesn't make Xander ache with frustrated longing. It feels good, warm. Like—family, maybe.

"All straightened out?" Justin asks, kissing Brooke's cheek.

"I think so," she says.

Xander snorts. "Nothing about me is straight, bro. You should know that by now."

Justin casually flips him off. "Okay, so you believe me?"

"I believe her," Xander retorts.

"Whatever. So now this is the part where you go over and grovel until he forgives you for being an asshole."

Xander blinks at the screen for the second time in maybe five minutes. "I—fuck. I have to go."

"Go get your man," Justin says, the last words cut off as Xander ends the call.

He bolts off the couch, cramming the phone into his pocket. Shoes—shoes are by the door. He grabs his coat out of the closet, gets the garage door open before he remembers his wallet, darts back to grab it off the coffee table.

The drive to Jordan's apartment has never taken so long, every light red. He sticks religiously to the speed limit, not willing to risk being pulled over. The whole time, though, there's a relentless drumbeat of *what if* in his head, doing its best to drown out the tiny fragile hope.

What if it's too late? What if Jordan isn't interested? What if he was, but after Xander's behavior today, he isn't anymore? What if he decides to wash his hands of the whole situation?

By the time he parks in the garage for Jordan's

building and punches in the keycode for the elevator, he's shaking on the inside, about to jitter out of
his skin with nervous energy. The elevator ride
seems to take forever and yet no time at all. Before
he knows it, he's standing in the hall outside of
Jordan's door.

Taking a breath, he summons the calm required
during a faceoff, overtime. Focus. *One way or
another, you'll know soon,* he tells himself.

He knocks.

18

JORDAN

Jordan's hand is on the doorknob, pulling his coat down off the hook with his other hand, when the knock sounds on the door. He stares blankly at it for a few seconds before turning the knob and opening it.

Give the day he's had, the last person he's expecting to see in the hallway is Xander. And yet, Xander is standing there, looking more frantic than Jordan's ever seen him, even when they're down by three at the start of the third, or headed toward overtime and probably a shootout. His hair is sticking up in all directions, like he's been running his hands through it repeatedly for hours. His t-shirt is probably a size too small and riddled with holes under his unzipped coat, his sweatpants have some indeterminate stain on the thigh and are almost worn through at the knees.

"I was an asshole," he blurts out, just as Jordan was opening his mouth to ask if everything was okay.

Jordan blinks. He wasn't expecting Xander to show up at his door, and he sure wasn't expecting those to be the first words out of his mouth. But, well, he's not wrong. "Yeah."

Xander laughs humorlessly, running a hand through his hair and making it stand up just the slightest bit more. "Yeah. Uh, can I come in? Or do you prefer me to do my groveling out here in the hall?"

"Oh, uh, yeah," Jordan steps back into the apartment, holding the door for Xander to come in, closing it behind him.

It's awkward in a way it hasn't been between them in weeks. Jordan's still pissed, but it's starting to fade, the edges of hurt hiding beneath the anger making themselves known, sharp and jagged. He leads the way to the couch, resolutely pushing the memories of other things they've done on the couch to the back of his mind.

Xander settles on the other end, his hands moving between his hair, his neck, and his knees with jerky, abortive motions. They sit like that, in silence, for a few minutes, while Xander opens his mouth, about to speak, then closes it again, then repeats the process.

"So, uh, like I said. I was an asshole today."

"No argument here." Jordan tries to keep his tone even, but he probably doesn't quite manage it. When the silence stretches again, he can't help but prod a little. "If that's all you came to say, you could've texted. Or called."

Xander's eyes shoot up to meet his, wide and half-panicked. "No, that's, I'm." He shakes his head. "I think I need to back up. Do you remember what I told you? Back when we first started hanging out?"

"You told me a lot of things."

"Yeah, I guess I did." He swallows, his face settling into determined lines. "I told you, after you said you were looking for a relationship, that I'd only ever felt that way about one person."

The knife in Jordan's heart twists a little deeper. "I remember," he says shortly. "You were very clear."

Xander shakes his head. "Not really. I didn't understand—I thought there was something wrong with me? Everybody else falls in love. I wasn't even sure what I was feeling was love. I just knew there was something broken inside me, that wouldn't let me feel those things."

Jordan forces himself not to reach out, to comfort. "There's a word for that, you know," he says, more gently than he'd planned.

"I do now," Xander agrees. "Aromantic. I was talking to Brooke, and she told me. I didn't—I didn't know there were other people who felt this way. But she told me about something else, another word that's better at fitting what I feel. Demiromantic."

He looks at Jordan expectantly, pausing to let that settle in.

"So you—" Jordan stops, because he's not exactly sure what the word means.

"I do sometimes fall in love, or feel romantic attraction," Xander says slowly, the words stumbling off his tongue a little. "But only with someone I have a previous connection with. Like a close friendship. And I dunno if you've noticed, but I don't exactly have a ton of those."

Jordan blinks. "What—what are you saying, here?"

"I'm saying I was an idiot and a dumbass and an asshole." Xander holds his gaze, eyes intent. "I woke up this morning, and you were there in my bed, on my pillow. All I could think about was that I wanted to wake up that way every day for the rest of my life."

"But—you left."

Xander nods. "I panicked. I thought that you deserved somebody better. Somebody who wasn't broken. Somebody who could love you like you wanted."

Jordan licks his lips, fighting down the hope surging up in his chest. "And now?"

"Now," Xander says slowly, "now I think maybe I can be that person. If you'll let me. If you'll give me another chance."

He takes a long, shaky breath. The only thing that lets him hold it together is that Xander looks just as wrecked as he feels. "I have one condition."

The smile that breaks across Xander's face is so bright it's almost blinding. "Anything. Name it."

Jordan reaches out, curling a hand around the back of Xander's neck and shaking him gently. "Never do that again. I need you to promise me. If you need space, time to be alone, maybe we had a fight, that's fine. Tell me or text me, or something, go do your thing. But don't ever ghost me again, okay?"

"I promise," Xander says as solemnly as possible when he's still smiling so widely. "Can I kiss you now?"

"I think that's what boyfriends do," Jordan says, returning the smile as he leans in.

It's hard to kiss when both people are smiling, teeth clacking together. Jordan gets his hand in Xander's hair, changes the angle a little, and the kiss goes soft, almost exploratory. They've kissed so many times; it's not that this feels like their first kiss. But it does feel different, a goal in itself instead of a step along the road to getting off.

It feels like a beginning.

EVENTUALLY, though, their kisses grow heated and urgent, tongues brushing together, hands sliding under clothes to find skin. Somehow Xander ends up in Jordan's lap, their shirts discarded who knows where as he makes a study of all the most sensitive places on Jordan's neck, comparing the responses from soft kisses and licks to the scrape of teeth and the rasp of stubble.

Jordan has to drag him away, eventually, because as good as this is—Xander's mouth on his skin,

Xander's hands brushing teasingly under the waistband of his pants, Xander's ass grinding down against his cock—he wants more. "Not here," he gasps, using the hand in Xander's hair to urge his head up. "We're not fucking teenagers, I'm not fucking you on the couch."

"That sounds like a challenge," Xander chirps back, but his smile is soft, even if he does roll his hips down one more time like the incredible tease he is. "But fine, I guess. Take me to bed, Darling."

A shiver that runs down Jordan's spine at that, the sound of his name in that rich, caressing voice. Xander's smile widens when he notices. "You like that?" he murmurs, sliding to his feet in one graceful motion and reaching down to pull Jordan up off the couch. "Want me to call you darling? Sweetheart? Honey? Baby?"

For a split second Jordan considers deflecting, but if they're doing this—if they're really doing this—he can't play it safe. "Yeah," he says quietly. "You can call me whatever you want, pretty boy."

"You already know I like that one." Xander leads him down the hallway and into the bedroom, face flushed when he glances back over his shoulder. "So what kind of sex do boyfriends have?"

"Whatever kind they want," Jordan retorts. He

spins Xander around when they stop next to the bed, pushing his sweatpants down over his hips. "What do you want, Xan?"

Xander swallows, holding his gaze. "I want you."

Jordan folds to his knees, pushing the sweatpants the rest of the way off, then running his hands back up Xander's legs to rest on his thighs. "I want to blow you."

"Fuck." Xander's cock twitches at the words, a bead of fluid appearing at the tip.

"And tomorrow," Jordan continues, leaning over to retrieve a condom and lube out of the drawer, "we're both gonna go get tested. Because I really want to blow you without one of these."

This time it's Xander's turn to shiver, the reaction rippling through his body as he sinks down to sit on the edge of the bed. "Yeah," he babbles, his hands clenching in the sheets. "Yeah, I—I want that. Too. I mean—"

The stream of words cuts off when Jordan rolls the latex down over his cock, lost in a long groan. He gets even louder when Jordan's mouth closes over the head, sliding slowly down.

"Fuck," he breathes, his knuckles going white in

Jordan's peripheral vision. "Fuck, Jordy, baby. That's so good. So—fuck. So good."

Jordan lifts his head long enough to say, "Tell me when you're close," before returning his attention to the task at hand. He's not quite sure how they haven't done this before, but somehow it's always been the other way around. He'd forgotten how much he loves doing this, the thick, pulsing weight on his tongue, the powerful rush of reducing a man to shaking muscles and incoherent, broken syllables.

Above him, Xander curses again. "I—fuck—I've been close, baby. Don't know how I lasted—shit—this long. God, your mouth feels fucking amazing—"

He whines when Jordan pulls back, hips arching up off the bed to try and follow.

"We're not done yet. Up on the bed," Jordan says, reaching for the lube and slicking up his hand.

Xander obeys without question, settling back against the pillows, his whole body taut with frustrated arousal. "What—"

"Shhh," Jordan soothes, climbing up and leaning in for a kiss. "Trust me, okay?"

"Oh—" Xander's voice breaks in the middle of the word when Jordan strips off the condom and strokes his cock with a slick hand, stroking slowly and deliberately up and down. "Okay."

It takes a few minutes of doing, but Jordan manages to nudge Xander thighs apart and settle between them. He leans down for another kiss, greedy now that he can do this as much as he wants, before sitting up to get a hand around both of their cocks. "Fuck," he groans, at the first slide of skin against skin.

"Yeah," Xander agrees breathlessly, his head thrown back against the pillow, hands coming up to clutch at Jordan's shoulders. He thrusts up as Jordan grinds down, meeting him stroke for stroke "Come on, baby, I'm so close—"

"Gonna come for me, pretty boy?" Jordan feels a little dizzy with the headiness of finally letting go, saying whatever he wants. "Always so fucking gorgeous when you come for me. Come on, I wanna see it. Come all over me, get me filthy, mark me up. I'm yours."

Xander's breath catches in his throat. "You too," he gasps, fingers digging in hard enough to bruise a little. "On me. All over me. I'm yours, too."

"Mine," Jordan agrees, breath coming faster. "Come on, Xan, let me see it, come on, baby—"

"Fuck!" Xander's eyes slide closed as he comes,

slick and hot all over Jordan's fist, his stomach and chest. The sight, the sensations, are overwhelming, and it only takes a couple of desperate thrusts before Jordan comes too, shuddering with the force of his orgasm.

When he can string thoughts together again, Xander is looking up at him, eyes soft in a way he doesn't think he's ever seen before.

"C'mere," Xander murmurs, tugging him down for a kiss, heedless of the mess between them. It's soft and sweet, the urgency gone and replaced with this spreading warmth.

They eventually have to break apart, but Xander holds him close when he tries to get up.

"We're a mess," Jordan protests half-heartedly. "We need to clean up."

"In a minute," Xander says, nuzzling his face into the side of Jordan's neck. "I want to enjoy this."

Jordan can't help smiling. "All right, but if we get stuck together with jizz I'm saying *I told you so.*"

"Fair, totally fair."

He lets himself relax into it, the comfort of Xander's hands rubbing up and down his back, skin on skin in a way that, for once, isn't sexual. It feels like comfort and belonging, all the things he didn't think he'd ever get to have with Xander.

They're still lying like that, some endless time later, when a thought floats into his head that has him laughing out loud.

"What?" Xander asks, his voice fuzzy in the way that means he's more than halfway to sleep.

"For once we're not playing a game on Thanksgiving this year," Jordan says, unable to stop smiling. "I'm just picturing what it'll be like when you come home with me and meet my Nana."

He's expecting panic or protests, and Xander does tense under him, but all he says is, "I'd like that."

Jordan leans up to kiss him again. "Me too."

19

XANDER

They bicker amiably about whose vehicle to take in the shower the next morning, but quickly get distracted by soapy hands sliding lazily over skin in a way that would have resulted in them being very late if they hadn't just come five minutes previously.

As it is, Xander's cock makes a valiant effort to get hard again. But he's not nineteen anymore, thank fuck, so he can focus on the simple comfort and intimacy of Jordan's skin under his hands. Of drying off and standing side-by-side at the double sinks as they brush their teeth and shave, of Jordan giving him shit for the amount of time he spends trying to make his hair look like he didn't just roll out of bed after getting fucked within an inch of his life.

"Hey, we can't all rock the buzz cut," Xander retorts, making a note to bring some duplicate products over next time he comes.

"I don't know," Jordan says easily, moving in behind him, arms wrapping around his waist. "I think you'd look hot with one."

Xander gives him a mock-scandalized look. "But my flow!"

Jordan sighs, his eyes crinkling at the corners as he tries not to smile. "I guess at least you wash it."

"Anyway," Xander says, finally admitting defeat on his hair and turning in the circle of Jordan's arms. "I think we should take my truck."

"But what if I need to go somewhere while you're at practice?" Jordan protests, but not very hard, his hands rubbing circles at the small of Xander's back.

It takes a supreme effort of will not to arch further into that touch, but Xander is a professional. He can focus. "You can get a Lyft if you need to; I'll put my account on your phone—"

"I can pay for my own shit," Jordan protests, a little more sharply than Xander was expecting."

"I know you can," he says cautiously. "But so can I. And if you're stuck at the arena with no vehicle because we took mine, it's only fair for me to pay."

Jordan looks like he's about to figure out the flaw in that argument, so Xander presses on without hesitating. "Besides. Mine has heated seats."

"Ugh, fine," Jordan says, but he's smiling again, leaning in for a kiss before he opens the closet door. "Do you want a clean shirt to wear to practice? Maybe one that isn't full of holes?"

Xander almost protests that they're going to have to swing by his house to pick up his gear anyway, but thinks better of it before the words make it out. "Yeah, that'd be good. Thanks."

He catches the t-shirt Jordan tosses him, soft from hundreds of washes, and pulls it on. It smells like Jordan, the familiar mingling of detergent and cologne, and he can't even be embarrassed when Jordan catches him taking a deep breath.

"Come on," Jordan says, smiling softly as he puts on his own clothes. "If we're going by yours, we need to get going or we're gonna be late."

"And coffee," Xander adds, hurrying to finish dressing.

They make the circuit in good time, grabbing Xander's gear bag from his house, driving through Starbucks where the barista hands his usual order through the window with a wink when she sees Jordan sitting next to him. Before he knows it, they're parked at the arena, stepping out of the truck.

"So, what—what are we doing here?" Jordan asks, stumbling over the words. "If you want to keep it quiet—"

"I don't," Xander interrupts, amazed that his hands are so steady. "If that's what you want, I won't like it, but we can—"

Jordan shakes his head. "No. No, I don't."

"Cool," Xander says. He hitches the strap of his bag further up onto his shoulder and switches his coffee to that hand before reaching out to Jordan with the other. "Then let's go."

There's only a moment's hesitation before Jordan laces their fingers together and they walk into the building, hand in hand.

MARIAN JUST NODS when they walk into the

trainers room together. "About fucking time, Jordy. If you'd dicked around any longer I was going to have to take drastic measures before someone else won the pool."

Jordan blinks at her. "You bet on me—us?"

"Wait, there's a pool?" Xander blurts out at the same time.

"You two have been too busy making googly eyes at each other to notice what's happening in front of your face," Marian scoffs, turning back to her desk. "Now get out of here, Richards, so we can do our job. And remember, if you fuck him over, they'll never prove it was me."

The threat is even more terrifying for the matter-of-fact tone in which it's delivered. Still not enough to keep Xander from leaning in and kissing Jordan goodbye, though, a lingering press of lips. "See you later, Darling," he murmurs, lifting his coffee in salute as he heads toward the door.

"Later," Jordan replies, the corners of his mouth curling up as he turns toward his desk.

Xander spares him one last backward glance as he turns toward the locker room. It's a little surprising, but he can't deny how much he's enjoying everything about this morning. The domesticity of waking up together, the frankly spectacular morning sex, driving in together, finally getting to kiss Jordan in public as much as he wants to.

Of course, the only thing that spreads faster than the common cold around here is gossip. By the time Xander makes it to the locker room, the news has clearly preceded him, judging by the flood of whoops and wolf whistles that greet him as he comes in the door.

"Nice hickey you've got there," Holtby calls from his stall. "Jordy must be a biter."

"Nah, Richie's not gonna kiss and tell anymore," Elvis drawls. "Not now that Jordy locked that down."

Xander just shakes his head and keeps walking, doing his best to ignore the rest of the comments while making his way to his stall. As soon as he sits down, though, Sasha is leaning over. "You are being good to him, yes? Treat him good?"

"Y-yeah, of course." Xander stumbles a little over the word in his surprise.

"Good." Sasha returns to strapping on his pads. "Keep that way, or they never find the body."

Xander blinks at him for a minute, but nothing else seems to be forthcoming, so he returns to putting on his own gear, only to be interrupted by Mac drifting over. "So, you and Jordy, huh?"

"Yeah," Xander answers cautiously. Not that Mac has ever been a dick about things, but this has been kind of a weird fucking morning.

"That's cool." Mac nods. "But like, you're serious about him, right? Not just a short-term thing?"

It takes Xander a minute to figure out how to even respond to that. "Not that it's anyone here's business," he says, raising his voice enough to carry, "but yes, I'm serious about Jordy. And he is about me."

"Good," David says, looking up from taping his socks. "Because if you fuck with him—"

"Yeah, yeah, they'll never find the body." Xander shakes his head. "Thanks, Cap. Is anybody giving *him* the shovel talk?"

The locker room fills with laughter. "Nah," Harty calls from his corner. "He has to deal with you; he's got enough on his plate without that."

Xander flips them off and goes back to gearing up, warmth blooming in his chest. It's not that he was nervous, not exactly, but some teams don't like people dating. Which is probably why David is watching Sasha and Mac laugh together out of the corner of his eye instead of joining them.

"You know," Xander says under the buzz of conversation, leaning in so only David can hear him. "You should go for it. You never know until you try."

David freezes for a minute, his whole body going stiff, then clearly forces himself to relax. "I don't know what you're talking about," he says, his voice equally quiet.

"Sure you don't." Xander pulls his jersey over his head. "And they don't spend as much time looking at you as you do at them."

"I don't—what?" David interrupts his practiced denial to gape blankly at Xander. "They don't—they're not."

Xander winks. "If I had to guess, I'd say they're waiting for you to make the first move. But like I said, you never know until you try."

David looks away. "One boyfriend and suddenly you're playing matchmaker," he mutters. "God help us when you two decide to get married."

"I—" It's Xander's turn to stumble over his words, but not for the reason David probably thinks. He's caught up in a mental picture of Jordan in a tux, reaching out to take Xander's hands, smiling a soft, private smile. It's an idea that should scare Xander, but instead he just feels—content. "Fine then. Be miserable instead of taking my perfectly good advice. I'm just saying, they wouldn't have a problem with you getting in there."

"Shut up, Richie," David mutters.

Xander raises his hands. "Whatever you say, Cap." He heads out to the ice before David can get another word it.

"LET me take a look at your shoulder before your nap," Jordan says as they walk into Xander's house that afternoon. "Just to be on the safe side."

"Not gonna argue with anything that gets your hands on me," Xander agrees, grinning back at him. "And then you can nap with me. New pre-game tradition."

Jordan shakes his head, but follows him into the bedroom. "I do have a job to do, you know."

"Awww, but I thought keeping me in shape was your job," Xander mock-pouts, doing his best to flutter his lashes.

"You're not the only player on the team,"

Jordan retorts, but he's smiling. "Come on, get your shirt off. You know you want to."

Xander stripped his shirt up over his head obediently, then pushed his basketball shorts and underwear down to fall on the floor. "How do you want me, Darling?"

"Sit your ass down," Jordan says, shaking his head again and pushing Xander down to sit on the edge of the bed before going back to retrieve a bottle of lotion and a towel from his bag.

When he gets back to the bed, Xander can't resist leaning in to steal a quick kiss.

"What was that for?" Jordan asks. He spreads the towel over the mattress behind Xander before pumping some lotion into his hands and starting to work on Xander's shoulder.

It's tricky to shrug with only one shoulder, but Xander does his best. "I just wanted to."

Jordan doesn't respond for a minute, apparently focusing his attention on Xander's shoulder, teeth digging into his lower lip. "Okay then," he finally says, sneaking a kiss of his own. "Lie down on your stomach."

Xander makes a show of stretching and crawling up until he can stretch out on the towel, smiling when he hears Jordan swear softly behind him.

There's a moment's hesitation, and then the mattress shifts underneath him as Jordan climbs up onto it.

"You're a menace, you know that?" Jordan's weight settles onto his ass, the fabric of his pants smooth and cool against Xander's bare skin. "Why do I put up with this?"

"You *like* me," Xander singsongs, but the last word dissolves into a groan as Jordan starts to work on his shoulder.

Jordan laughs, his hands slick and warm on Xander's skin. "For some reason. I guess your face is all right."

"Not what you were saying last night—fuck!" Xander presses his forehead to the mattress and takes a deep breath, trying to stay relaxed, not tense up and ruin all Jordan's work.

"Shh, I got you, baby," Jordan murmurs absently. His hands are relentless, searching out every knot and pain point in Xander's shoulder. It's a massage like any other, except for the pet names. Except for the fact that Xander is lying here, naked and vulnerable, his cock doing it's level best to remind him of how things ended the last time Jordan gave him a massage in a bed.

Eventually Jordan's touch eases, but instead of

stopping as usual, he works his way across to Xander's other shoulder, gently but firmly kneading at the muscles there until Xander feels like he's melting into the mattress, warm and relaxed. His cock is still hard, but it seems like too much effort to try and do anything about it. He's drifting in that blissful headspace when Jordan's touch starts moving slowly down his back, finding the last lingering bits of tension and releasing them.

He wakes up a little when Jordan's weight lifts off of him, but he's just nudging Xander's thighs apart and settling to the mattress between them. He continues the massage, down Xander's left leg to the sole of his feet—"marry me," Xander slurs into the mattress, and Jordan just laughs—then repeats the process on his right.

Just when Xander thinks it's over, Jordan's hands land on his ass, kneading the muscle there and spreading him wide. He's suddenly, intensely hard, incredibly awake and aware of every touch, the way Jordan's thumbs slide so teasingly close to his hole, the press of each individual finger into his skin.

"As soon as those test results come back," Jordan murmurs, "I'm gonna get my mouth on you, eat you out until you come for me."

"Fuck," Xander groans, his hips grinding down helplessly into the mattress from the mental picture. "Fuck, Jordy, please—"

He can hear the smile in Jordan's voice. "Don't worry, baby, I've got you."

When a slick digit brushes over his hole, he pushes back into it, but Jordan braces an arm over the small of his back, pinning him to the bed. "None of that," Jordan chides softly, rubbing teasing circles over the sensitive skin, never quite pushing inside. "You need to be rested for your game tonight. Just lie there and let me take care of you."

"I didn't realize killing me with sexual frustration counted as taking care of meee—" Xander's snark cuts off on a moan when the tip of Jordan's finger finally, finally slips inside. "More, fuck, please, more."

"So greedy," Jordan's mock-chiding would be a whole lot more effective if he wasn't sounding pretty breathless himself, if his voice wasn't so much lower than usual. "Come on, baby, let me make you feel good."

Xander huffs out a breath, but it's hard to stay petulant when Jordan's finger is sliding inside him so easily, long and thick and *not enough*. "Your cock makes me feel good."

"Soon," Jordan promises, adding a second finger. "I don't want to hurt you."

"I'm not fragile," Xander grumbles. It's not that he's not enjoying this, because he sure as fuck is. But as much as he loves being pinned to the bed and fucked within an inch of his life, he's used to being a more active participant in sex.

Jordan pumps his fingers in and out, stretching him open. "I know you aren't," he says quietly. "But—I want to. Let me?"

"Whatever you want," Xander concedes, letting himself relax into the bed that last bit.

When Jordan adds a third finger, he leans down and leaves little teasing, biting kisses on the curve of each ass cheek. A reminder, a promise, of what they both want him to do. The thought of it, of Jordan licking him wet and open, is enough to send a shudder racing down Xander's spine.

Before he has too long to dwell on it, though, there's the sound of a foil packet being ripped open, a wet, obscene noise that can only be Jordan slicking up his cock. He pulls his fingers out slowly, curling them so the tips drag over Xander's prostate. Before Xander has time to lament the emptiness,

Jordan lines himself up and starts pushing slowly inside.

Xander fists his hands in the sheets. "Fuck," he breathes.

Jordan is inexorable, never stopping until his hipbones are pressed up against Xander's ass. He leans down to kiss the back of Xander's neck. "Need a minute?"

"I need you to fuck me," Xander retorts, his voice embarrassingly breathless. "C'mon, baby, please?"

A slight retreat, and then Jordan pushes back in. "Like that?"

Xander tries to roll his hips up, get him deeper, but he has no leverage like this. "More, please, come on—"

"More what?" Jordan teases, grinding into him with tiny, shallow thrusts. "More of this?"

"Harder. Faster." It sends that shiver down his spine again, having no recourse but to ask for what he wants. Except it's even better than that time with a random stranger, because this is Jordan. They can do this whenever they want. "Please, baby, I want you to fuck me."

Jordan keeps up that slow, maddening grind. "I am fucking you, baby. You don't think you can come like this?"

Every movement rubs Xander's cock between his belly and the towel, the friction so good, just the right side of too rough, but not enough. "No, no, I can't," he babbles. "I need more, please."

"Like this?" Jordan pulls out partway, then drives back in with a snap of his hips, somehow managing to unerringly nail Xander's prostate. "That what you want, baby?"

"Fuck." The word sobs out of Xander's throat, broken in the middle as Jordan repeats the movement. "Yes, please, fuck, don't stop, don't stop—"

Jordan presses down on top of him, kissing between his shoulder blades. "I'm not gonna stop, baby. Not till you come for me. Think you can do that?"

Xander's only reply is a wordless noise. His orgasm builds at the base of his spine, stealing his breath with every unrelenting stroke of Jordan's cock against that sensitive spot inside him. He has no idea how many it takes until he comes—all he knows is that he comes, helplessly, and that Jordan keeps moving inside him, fucking him through it, until he shudders and goes still.

He must doze off, because one moment they're lying there, breathing hard, hearts thundering under their skin, and the next thing he knows is Jordan's weight shifting off him. He manages a vague noise of complaint, but can't bring himself to stir from his place on the bed.

"I'll be right back," Jordan murmurs. Fortunately Xander's head is turned the right way to watch him walk into the bathroom, because even in his current puddle-like state, that's a view he doesn't think he'll ever get tired of.

The front view when Jordan comes back, washcloth in hand is pretty good, too. "You're pretty," Xander mumbles, too close to sleep to be embarrassed by the words.

Jordan laughs softly. "Don't think I'm the pretty one in this relationship. Come on, roll over. Let's get you cleaned up."

"Nooo," Xander protests, making no effort to move. "Can't move. Sleep."

"If you sleep like that, you're gonna wake up stuck to the towel." Jordan nudges at him until he rolls unwillingly onto his back, twitches the soiled towel out from under him and wipes him down with the washcloth. "There. Get your nap now."

Xander sticks his lower lip out in the most exaggerated pout he's ever used in his life. "Stay with me?"

Jordan sighs, wrapping the towel and washcloth into a bundle. "I literally signed up for this."

"Yeah." Xander does his best to figure out how to pull the covers up from the twisted mess at the end of the bed without moving from his comfortable spot.

Finally Jordan grabs them with another sigh, settling them over Xander before sliding in beside him. "Fine. Get some sleep so you don't get me fired."

Xander falls asleep before he can string enough words together to respond.

THE MOOD in the locker room is good, electric and confident. Xander tapes his stick, settles his gear, listens to the coaching staff and David outline their strategy. The Abs are having a rough time this season; they lost too many veterans in trades for draft picks that won't pay off for awhile, their talent still too green to make up for the lack of experience. Which sucks for them, but that's how it goes sometimes.

Speeches over, everyone gets to their feet, ready to file out into the tunnel, head toward the ice or the bench. As usual, there's a little bit of a traffic jam at the door, so Xander has plenty of time to cross the room to where Marian and Jordan stand in the corner.

"Kiss for luck?" he asks as soon as he gets into earshot.

Jordan's eyes go wide, looking around to see who heard, and Marian just shakes her head. Somebody mock-whispers, "Get it, Richie," from across the room, but Xander just waits.

"You're not going anywhere, are you?" Jordan mutters under his breath.

Xander grins at him. "See, I knew you were the smart one in this relationship. Besides, this might be your last chance to kiss me with all my original teeth."

Jordan rolls his eyes and pecks him perfunctorily on the lips.

"Thanks, honeybunch," Xander calls back over his shoulder as he joins the line headed out the door.

Coach White shoots him a narrow-eyed look as he gets closer. "Are we going to need to talk about this, Richards?"

"No, sir," Xander gestures a little salute with his stick. "I'm ready to play hockey."

"Good." White turns his attention to something Johnson shows him.

Xander walks out into the tunnel, inhales the smell of the ice, lets the roar of the crowd wash over him, and glides into the arena with Jordan's kiss still tingling on his lips.

ABOUT THE AUTHOR

Ariel Bishop is an American romance and erotica author who feels strongly that all love triangles are best resolved through healthy polyamory. She lives in the Ozarks with her partners, their children and two bunnies that rejoice in the names Reginald von Pancakes and Snickers.

More information about her books can be found at her website or by signing up for her mailing list. You can also find her on Tumblr, Twitter, and Facebook. For sneak previews of upcoming books in the Tripping series and other rewards, you can support her on Patreon or Gumroad.

Keep reading for a list of her other works and a sneak peek at book 2 in the Tripping series, *Three-Man Advantage*!

THREE-MAN ADVANTAGE SNEAK PEEK

Enjoy a sneak peek from Three-Man Advantage, *Book 2 in the Tripping Series, coming June 2018!*

David

"Hey, Cap."

David looks up from unlacing his skates when he hears the familiar voice. Sasha must have taken advantage of David staying behind to help Ray with his backhand, because he's freshly showered, dark hair damp and curling behind his ears and at the nape of his neck, stray water droplets clinging to his bare chest—David tears his eyes away.

By now he should be used to Sasha's habit of

wandering around the locker room wearing only a very small towel, if that. It's not like he's the only one—at least half the Wendigos are shameless nudists. But with most of them, David has no trouble looking away. Yes, hockey creates attractive bodies, but there are only a few cases where David feels the magnetic pull, the need to stare.

"Hey," he says back, returning his attention to the laces he's managed to knot together, trying to ignore Sasha's muscular thighs in his peripheral vision. "What's up?"

"Mac says I should talk to you about party," Sasha says, settling down on the bench next to him. "How we can help, all that."

The stubborn laces finally come apart, and David shucks his skates off before starting on the rest of his gear. It's stupid to feel shy about it, but between Sasha sitting so close and Mac watching from the goalie stall at the end, he feels caught, self-conscious in a way he hasn't since his first Juniors locker room.

"The Thanksgiving party, right," he says, voice muffled as he pulls the practice jersey off over his head. "I know, Connolly, I know, *American* Thanksgiving."

"I'm just saying," Con mutters, loud enough to be heard all around the locker room, as usual.

David can't help grinning, the normalcy of the exchange helping him feel more settled in his skin. "Tell you what, Con, you convince the CHL to make Canadian Thanksgiving a holiday and we'll do two parties. But until then, we're in Wisconsin, so suck it up and be thankful that we're not actually playing that day."

"Amen," Dino chimes in as he heads out the door. "Make sure you have pumpkin pie, Cap."

"You'll eat what we have and you'll like it," David calls after him.

Sasha laughs quietly next to him. "So, you have plan? Or we need make plan?"

"I have—part of a plan," David admits. "We should probably sit down and go over it, but I'm gonna hit the showers first. I stink."

He realizes his mistake when Sasha leans in even closer, the tip of his nose just barely brushing David's neck, and inhales. "Smell fine to me," Sasha murmurs, a barely audible rumble compared to his usual booming voice. "But go, keep Mac company."

David is too busy trying to escape before Sasha notices his reaction to parse that last statement until he makes it into the showers, empty except for Mac. Of fucking course.

"Hey, Cap." Mac turns his back to the spray, closing his eyes as he tips his head back to wet his hair. "Sash and I were thinking lunch? We can go over the party plans and stuff our faces at the same time."

"Sounds good." David hopes his voice isn't as choked as it sounds in his own ears, but the universe is clearly conspiring against him. Going from Sasha's half-naked proximity to this, water cascading down over Mac's compactly muscled chest—fuck. "What were you guys thinking? Sushi?"

Mac shrugs, opening his eyes and reaching for the soap. "Works for me. I'll check with Sash when I get back out there. You want to ride with us?"

"I can meet you," David says, doing his best to concentrate on cleaning himself off and not the lazy movements of Mac's hands over his skin. The last thing he needs when he's this on edge is to be crammed into the middle seat of Mac's ridiculous pickup truck. "I have some errands I need to run after."

"Whatever works."

Mac steps out from under the spray, grabbing a

towel and scrubbing it over his hair and body before wrapping it loosely around his waist and disappearing in the direction of the locker room.

David slumps against the wall for a second, just breathing. The locker room showers aren't the ideal place to give himself a pep talk, but it looks like this is where it needs to happen.

You are an adult man, he tells himself, reaching for the soap and scrubbing over his skin with impatient motions. *You are going to go have lunch with your alternate captains who are also your best friends. You are going to plan the best Thanksgiving party this team has ever seen. You will not ogle them or get lost in thought trying to figure out if they're actually together or just really good friends. Then you will go home, take your nap, come back here, and play some damn good hockey.*

He thinks darkly, as he dries himself off and heads back into the locker room to get dressed, that this is all Xander's fault. Ever since he started dating Jordan, the team's massage therapist, he's been gently poking at David, trying to get him to make a move. Which is just ridiculous. The pool on whether or not Mac and Sasha are together has never actually been won. Either they're very good at keeping things under wraps, or there's nothing going on.

But even if they are together, there's no reason to think that they, what, would welcome David in? That's not—normal people don't do that. David has long ago resigned himself to the stupidity of being attracted to both of his alternate captains. But he's not willing to risk the humiliation of opening himself up to rejection from two people at the same time. He may play hockey, but that doesn't make him a masochist.

Get early chapters of Three Man Advantage *and other perks by supporting Ariel on Patreon!*

www.ingramcontent.com/pod-product-compliance
Lightning Source LLC
Chambersburg PA
CBHW050553190726
48283CB00007B/2116